"Can I buy you a drink?"

Her eyes were dark as starless nights and her summer-petal lips bloomed full. Her coal-colored hair, tightly woven into a short braid, was a backdrop to her ginger-tinted skin. An island woman.

"Sex on the beach," I replied with a seductive smile.

"Excuse me?"

How long I had waited for this moment, to ask for this drink, simply to say its name. I'm not a drinker, had no idea what was in it, but the words, *sex on the beach,* had their implications. The woman blushed.

When a butch woman blushes, she crosses a subtle boundary. Momentarily out of control, she lets go. It's like orgasm. When I make a butch woman blush, it's almost as sweet as making her come.

"Sex on the beach? Is that a drink or a suggestion?" She laughed.

Her eyes locked into mine then drifted to my breasts where they brazenly lingered. I felt heat simmer between my legs as she appraised what I had to offer. Out-of-towner, easy girl, seated on a bar stool, waiting for my drink.

About the Author

Robbi Sommers was born in Cincinnati, Ohio in 1950. She lives in Northern California where she divides her time between Dental Hygiene, motherhood, and writing. The author of the bestselling *Pleasures, Players, Kiss and Tell, Behind Closed Doors, Personal Ads,* and *Getting There,* she shyly admits to "liking a good time."

Kiss & Tell

BY ROBBI SOMMERS

The Naiad Press, Inc.
1997

Printed in the United States of America on acid-free paper
First Edition
Second Printing, June 1992
Third Printing, December 1994
Fourth Printing, February 1997

Edited by Christine Cassidy and Katherine V. Forrest
Cover design by Pat Tong and Bonnie Liss
    (Phoenix Graphics)
Typeset by Sandi Stancil

Library of Congress Cataloging-in-Publication Data

Sommers, Robbi, 1950–
    Kiss and tell / by Robbi Sommers.
        p.   cm.
    ISBN 1-56280-005-1
    I. Lesbians—Fiction.   2. Erotic stories, American.   I. Title.
PS3569.065335K57   1991
813'.54—dc20   91-25238
                                                                      CIP

For Cindy . . .
The sweetest *Sin*

Thank you for inspiration:
Women who take me with their eyes
Women with attitude
The meanest Mommy
The sweetest Daddy
Nasty girls who do
Nasty girls who did
Ruby
Sin
Krysta
And my muse who knows quite well . . .

Author's Note

Within the context of fiction, I have not included safe sex practices between my characters. Crossing the line from fiction to reality, I strongly promote safe sex.

Books by Robbi Sommers

Pleasures

Players

Kiss and Tell

Uncertain Companions

Behind Closed Doors

Personal Ads

Getting There

Between the Sheets (Audio Book)

Contents

Kiss And Tell

You want the truth? I'll give you the truth.
I like sex.
Soft and sweet, hard and rough —
I like sex.
Any way I can think of, any place I can think of,
Any woman who catches my eye —
I like sex.
Oh yes, I'll give you the truth.

The women I meet? I want to skip the small
talk, take them to my car and pull their pants

down. I want to see them with their legs spread. I want to see it all. I want to overstep boundaries.

I want to have affairs with married women, flirt with inappropriate people. I want to memorize women's phone numbers while my girlfriend smiles from the bar. I want to break rules.

I want to be surrounded by a gang of biker women. I want them to admire me, tease me, rip my blouse, raise my skirt. I'll play scared, but love it all. I want to walk the edge.

I want sex toys, crazy toys, take-them-out-and-use-them toys. Smuggled from the tool chest, the kitchen, my job — I'll hide them in my bedroom. And later, I'll push them, slowly, deep inside. I want to be nasty.

There's a woman, half my age, who says I scare her. I want to take her, dismay her, overawe and then delight her. I want to get her in bed, take her in my arms and smother her with unharnessed passion. I want to cross barriers.

I want to love and leave, leave and love. Be cool, be hard, be butch, be dangerous. I want twosomes, threesomes, sex with strangers, sex with best friends.

The more comfortable I am with myself, the more I want discomfort. I want to call my ex-lover, tempt my ex-lover, seduce, get wild, devour my ex-lover — just because I shouldn't. I want to push limits.

I want a woman to watch as my lover fucks me. I want to hear my lover tell her how I like it — how sweet my pussy is, how pretty my pussy is, how drop-dead hot my pussy is.

I want women to look at me and wonder if I'm wild. I want them to watch as I get wild for them. I want to be blindfolded, held down, taken and loved.

2

I want to be opened up, shut down, turned on and turned out.

I want to take my chances, walk the line. I'll flaunt like a sex goddess, strut like a cop, instruct like a teacher, entice like a whore. Harsh in a business suit, smooth in a black dress, I'll boast in leather, I'll tease in lace.

I want it all — a bad girl, a rebel girl, a sweet girl, a good girl, a wild-haired femme, a tough-assed butch — I want it all.

This is my time, this is my decade. I want to show up, show off, and then show how. I want to do it up, then write it down.

I kiss and tell.

A Job Well Done

Even with the recession, my janitorial business does just fine. I take pride in my work and I'm unrelenting. I don't quit until a job's done — and done right.

Recently, Dr. Claxton offered me big bucks to give his dental office a weekly once-over. The guy's a sweetheart. Shit, if I wasn't so fucking scared of dentists, I'd make an appointment there myself. But I hate going to the dentist, hate the smell, hate the music, hate the sounds, and if nothing hurts, I don't go. Period.

But money's money and I figured that as long as I didn't have to open my mouth, the place was quiet and Dr. Claxton came up with the big check at the end of the week, I could find my way to clean the place.

Since the setup for this gig was seven rooms, I signed on Marci to give me a hand. With an assistant, I could still pull a sweet bankroll, have someone to bullshit with and finish the job in half the time.

The fine print of the situation read like this: Marci was more of a looker than a scrubber — one glance at her lily-smooth hands told me that. Although Loraine wanted the job and would have busted ass for me, the combination of Marci's flirtatious attitude, the way her jeans fit her round ass, the moon lingering in Scorpio — shit, I was pussy-struck. Marci got the job, hands down.

When Marci and I got to Dr. Claxton's Thursday evening, we started the job, pronto. I rolled my sleeves in the bathroom and Marci headed for the back rooms. With Marci's help, I was looking at two hours, max. Even so, I hustled to get the job wrapped. Marci had been sending me electro-charged signals since she climbed into my truck. If I played my hand nice and smooth, by the end of the evening, I'd have Marci in a royal flush.

I was scrubbing the floor, minding my own business, when I heard Marci call.

"Doctor?"

Damn. I figured Dr. Claxton had made an appearance to do a look-see. I fucking hate it when an owner noses around a job. I tucked my rag into my back pocket, tightened the bandanna around my forehead and opened the restroom door. The office was dark except for a light streaming from a back room.

"Shit," I mumbled. The last thing I wanted was to waste my time talking shop with the Doc.

"Marci?"

"In here," she called.

"Marci, is Dr. Claxton . . . ?" I barely breezed into the room when I jammed on the brakes. There, in the dental chair, sat Marci, stripped to the buff.

"Doctor, thank God you've made it. I have such a terrible, terrible ache," Marci cooed dramatically.

Sizing up the situation, I shot Marci a look — lingering hungrily on her cherrystone nipples then sliding to her neatly trimmed pussy fur.

"I don't know," Marci said as she separated her legs slightly. "One moment I was fine, the next I had this throbbing."

A flash of pink teased between her well-manicured pussy lips and a stab of hard heat shot through me. Damn, she was fucking beautiful with her creamy skin and her tongue gliding over her pouty coral mouth.

"Throbbing, huh?" I touched her forehead real light. "You gotta fever?"

"Do I feel hot?" she purred.

I cupped her breast and tugged the flushed point between my fingers. "Yeah, you feel pretty damn hot," I said.

The nipple buckled into a deep rose square. I pressed the hardened cube between my fingers and Marci moaned.

"Oh Doctor, Doctor," Marci gasped. "The throbbing is unbearable. Perhaps you should . . ." She handed me a small mouth mirror.

Marci, Marci, Marci, I thought. My clit was pounding in time with my heart.

"Open wide," I said with a professional flair.

Marci, sweet as candy, spread her legs. Her pussy lips separated like tiny brown curtains and her coral flesh was prominently visible between them.

"Where, exactly, does it hurt?" I said, short-breathed.

"Right here." She sighed innocently. She V-ed her fingers between the lips, parting them further. Her plump clit hung in flappy pleats, providing a luscious backdrop for the swollen red jewel it housed.

I could read Marci, and there was no question — she wanted it bad. She was ready as a hotcake on a silver platter. Not one to sit on my ass, I adjusted the overhead light. The bright beam spotlighted her pretty pink package. I tapped the small mirror against her clit.

"Right there, Missy?"

A silver dew glistened on her pink lower lips. Dipping the mirror between them, I circled it against her rimmed slit.

"Yes, right there, Doctor."

"As I suspected," I said thickly. My mouth moistened at the sight of her showy pussy. My heart raced as images, countless images, passed through my mind. Oh the things, the nasty hot things, I could do with this pussy!

The seam of my pants, flush against my own swollen pussy, was sopping wet. I had aches, I had insistent throbbings of my own to contend with. I pushed the mirror into her buttery cunt and twisted the handle. Yeah, the mirror would turn, the mirror would push against her tight walls, would force them to separate. Oh the things I could do!

Marci pushed a switch and the head portion of her chair tilted way down, the leg portion out. What a delicious sight she was. Her sweetness spread before me, lifted as though on an altar.

Breathless, I pulled the mirror from the red-hemmed slit. I could feel her muscles tighten to hold the mirror but her well-toned grip was no match for my strong hands. With a quick tug, I plucked the mirror from her rebel cunt.

The silver glass was slathered with a thick coat of shimmering sugar. Without a thought, I dipped the mirror into my mouth and sucked the honey glaze. She was the sweetness of a bee's pursuit laced with a slightly tart edge. Her taste made my knees tremble.

I could have sunk my tongue and lapped her, buried my lips against her berry-clustered clit, sucked her until I popped her off. But I kept my cool, slowed my clip.

Next to the chair, barely covered by a white napkin, were the things, those frightening silver things, that had kept me from the dentist's chair all these years. Yet tonight, as they sparkled on the tray, they looked irresistibly inviting.

The sprayer and suction tube rested provocatively

in black hoops on the tray's edge. I grabbed the sprayer gadget and pushed the flat button on top. A stream of water shot across the room.

"Is the area sensitive to cold?" I asked. My voice was steady, but inside, I shivered with passion.

"I'm not certain, Doctor," Marci said as she arched her hips. She kept her succulent pussy spread wide for me.

"Perhaps we should test the area?" I shot a stream of water directly onto her pussy.

Marci's hips jolted and water spurt in all directions. But who the fuck cared? I pushed both buttons on top of the sprayer and the water blasted with air. The pressure forced the bulbous tissue away from her beet-red clit point.

Spellbound by her hardened rough marble, hypnotized as the nugget hung from the tissues like a tiny ripened cherry, I kept blasting the water.

Marci rotated her hips. She moaned, she cried, she pleaded. She was crazy, a wild tiger.

"Oh, yeah! Oh, yeah!" She panted as she stretched her lips apart.

Her clit head struggled in a hopeless match with the water pressure. Marci wanted it, hurt for it. Her clit twitched in hungry spasms. God, there was nothing like pussy. Nothing, nothing, nothing.

"Doctor, don't stop," Marci begged.

Oh, but I had to stop. What a nasty, nasty mess the procedure had caused. It had been a long time since my last bout in a dental chair, but I remembered, all too well, what had to be done.

"Gotta dry the area," I said quickly. "Open wide."

The suction turned on with a twist of a dial and I began to suck the water from between her wet legs. Rotating her pussy in small circles, Marci egged me on.

It didn't take much to get me started. I could only take so much of her pouting clit's insistent taunting. I angled the suction tip against her clit pouch. The open end of the suction tip tried to swallow in her pulpy tissue.

Marci yelped, but shit, it didn't sound like she was asking me to stop. I pressed her clit, caught the flesh, then lightly lifted the whole fucking thing. The tip grasped her tissue unmercifully. I pumped up and down and her entire pussy swelled like a small pink balloon.

"Area looks dried," I said as I snapped the tip, breaking the suction from her clit. "Almost too dry."

I tapped my finger against her thick shaft and Marci jerked.

"Still sensitive, huh?" I pulled the napkin from the tray and did a quick once over of the silver tools. "Gotta get rid of the hypersensitivity, Missy."

Topical Anesthetic — the words on a small bottle caught my eye. It was the only sensible way I could think to relieve poor Marci's discomfort. I sank my finger into the gel and smoothed a thin coating against the obviously inflamed area in question.

"Holy shit!" Marci bolted forward as she grabbed her mink-furred lips.

Pressing my mouth onto hers, I pushed her back into the chair.

"Go with it. Ride it out, baby," I whispered as I kissed her deep.

She struggled beneath me but never stopped kissing me. Women like her liked it this way, a little out of their control. She moved her tongue in

11

my mouth like she never had it so good. Yeah, her pussy probably stung, but she knew it was temporary, had to be done.

I grabbed the arms of the chair and the whole fucking chair started to move up and down. Yeah, up and down we went as her pussy stung, as I sucked her mouth, as she dug her teeth into my lip.

Enough of this, I thought wildly. There were certain things, there were certain procedures, that had to be done.

I reached for the tooth polisher. Holding the gadget, I playfully fingered the rubber cup wondering how the hell to make it work. I pushed buttons with no luck. Stepping back, I accidentally hit a floor pedal. To my delight, the rubber cup began to swirl.

"Still aching, baby?"

Marci got crazy. She spread her pussy and worked her piece with her hands — like I wasn't going to do her stuff right, like I wasn't going to pop her hard.

"Take it easy, baby," I demanded, but Marci was bucking like she was on hot coals. From the look of her lava-red pussy, I had to agree.

"I can't, I can't, I can't," Marci cried.

I pushed her hips down, pulled her hands aside and started the rubber polisher. Nice and easy, I thought. Nice and fucking easy.

Spreading those femmy lips of hers, I carefully grazed the edge of the rubber tip on her clit. Marci grabbed my arm and dug her whitened fingers into my skin. I barely felt her. My body was charged beyond touch.

Around and around the little cup turned. I held her tight, I held her open. Her clit-bead glistened in the light like a ruby. She was ready, she was on her way. I ran the cup, teased the cup, against her clit. Up and down, soft and faster, I tapped the shaft, I tickled the folds.

Marci started to come so I backed off. She could wait. She could wait until I was ready. I poked the suction tip into her cunt and turned it on. Dragging it out, I angled the tip toward her G-spot. Yeah, I'd suck that baby till she shot off, all right. I grazed the rubber cup, sweet and easy, then backed it with the suction's slight, persistent tugs.

Marci started to come off hard, which was fine with me. She scraped the shit out of my arm, screamed for me to stop. I kept it up, unrelenting, until I finished the job I'd started, and finished it right.

Friday, Dr. Claxton gave me a bonus, twenty-five bucks. He said he'd never had a service do his office so well. I couldn't agree more.

Extra Credit

The qualifications for acceptance into medical school were strict and Marla Trester could not afford less than a four-point average in her premed classes. And until this semester, until Histology, things had looked favorable.

With only a few weeks left in the semester, Marla's grade was a concrete B. No matter how hard she studied for the tests, she never could raise her grade to an A. Concerned, Marla scheduled a meeting with Dr. Anderte, her professor, and explained her predicament.

"Your only option at this point," Dr. Anderte said unsympathetically, "is to do extraordinarily well on the final."

"I can't imagine studying any harder than I already do," Marla said, not hiding her frustration. "When I sit for the exams, I'm sure I know the material, but somehow . . ."

Dr. Anderte's pencil made a slight clicking sound as she tapped it against her desk. Although a handsome woman, her graying hair, twisted severely into a tight bun, created a harsh edge to her face.

"Perhaps there is one other option." Dr. Anderte pushed at the black-framed glasses that had slipped down her angular nose. "Not standard, mind you, but with the circumstances being such as they are . . . your entire future hinges on this one grade . . ."

"I'll do anything," Marla said quickly.

Dr. Anderte's glasses had, again, slid down her nose and she peered over the rims at Marla. "Yes," she said dryly. "I suppose you would."

Research credit, Professor Anderte had explained, meant pledging four hours of her time as an in-class assistant to Dr. Anderte. This particular class consisted of fourteen women medical students. Marla would assist Dr. Anderte as needed and in return, her grade would be raised to "the A she so deserved but never quite achieved."

Marla sat in the front row of the med school's amphitheater and listened as Dr. Anderte lectured the small group. Dressed in a white lab coat, her hair tucked into her characteristic bun, Dr. Anderte discussed gynecological considerations in the complete patient exam.

Referring to chart after chart, she illustrated various techniques used for pelvic exams. Marla, with the rest of the class, was engrossed in her detailed descriptions.

"And now —" Dr. Anderte glanced toward Marla — "I'd like to walk the class through a complete gynecological exam."

Marla felt suddenly uneasy and involuntarily averted her eyes.

"Marla, if you would come forward." Dr. Anderte motioned to her.

The amphitheater seemed unnaturally quiet as Marla walked toward the center of the room.

"There's a dressing gown in that closet." She pointed to a small door near the exit.

Marla asked vaguely, "Am I the one you're —"

"We are striving for a four-point are we not?" Dr. Anderte interrupted, her voice low, yet stern.

Marla nodded. After all, she reasoned, she needed the A in Histology. In another year she would be a second-year med student, sitting in this very amphitheater.

In the small closet, flanked by cotton robes and lab coats, Marla exchanged her clothes for a light green gown. She knotted the front ties and returned to the amphitheater.

"Fine, Marla," Dr. Anderte said casually, gesturing to an examination table that had been moved to the center of the room. "If you would . . ."

Marla climbed onto the table and sat quietly as Dr. Anderte addressed the class. The med students,

17

separated in low tiers, sat directly across from Marla. The lights now seemed hotter, brighter, than when Marla had been in the audience. And as Dr. Anderte moved closer, Marla noticed a thin layer of perspiration above the doctor's upper lip.

Dr. Anderte pressed Marla's shoulder and guided her back against the exam table. "Once the legs are positioned, like so —" She navigated Marla's feet into the stirrups. "We have the patient relax her knees to each side. Yes, thank you, Marla."

"Grace, if you would," Dr. Anderte said, resting her arm precariously close to Marla's face. So close that Marla was invaded by the sharp floral scent of her cologne.

A woman, holding a video camera, stepped to the end of the examination table.

"As you can see on the screens," Dr. Anderte said, nodding toward the TV sets that hung from the ceiling, "I will be using a magnifying lens so you can observe, in complete detail, the procedure."

Marla glanced at a monitor. A close-up of her dark matted pubic hair flashed onto the screen. Oh God, she thought, embarrassed. She closed her eyes and turned her face.

"As I discussed earlier, the labia majora can vary in size. As we can see here —" Dr. Anderte used a thin wooden stick to tap the thick folds that completely covered Marla's pinkness — "Our patient today has rather large lips."

The class was quiet except for an occasional rustling of papers or a random clearing of the throat.

"Overlarge labia majora don't necessarily mean that the vulva itself will be bulky. In fact, often enough, it's difficult to know what to expect when the lips are pulled open."

Dr. Anderte paused, taking a moment to push her glasses up on her nose. The film of perspiration had aggravated the chronic problem she had with her glasses.

The air of anticipation felt thick, yet it seemed that Dr. Anderte took a covert delight in hesitating before exposing the inner secrets of a patient's most private cache. After all, Marla thought, it must be a privilege to be a party to such a personal examination and Marla was sure Dr. Anderte always tried to show her patients the utmost respect in these circumstances.

"I suspect," Dr. Anderte said as she broke the momentary silence, "that our patient today has a vulva that is on the fleshier side. Notice, if you will, that toward the bottom of the labia majora — Grace, please angle in on this shot — there is the very hint of the labia minora."

The class shifted as though trying to get a better look at the TV screens.

"You see, right here, the very edge of the inner lips." Dr. Anderte pried the blunt end of the stick between the lower part of the outer lips. She lightly teased the pink tissue that peeked provocatively between them. "Can you all see clearly?"

The class mumbled in discontent. Yes, they could see, but clearly? No, not clearly enough.

Dr. Anderte, seemingly oblivious to the class's

dissatisfaction, continued on with her lecture. "As we separate the labia minora, we undrape the vulva pulp."

Marla felt Dr. Anderte's gloved fingers stretch her open.

"Always apply a lubricant before contact with the genital flesh. A dry working field not only creates discomfort for the patient, but also an unnatural resistance to the practitioner's fingers."

The doctor squirted an oily gel across Marla's wide open pussy. Marla arched involuntarily as the surprisingly cold jelly spurted onto her clitoris. She saw, displayed on the screens around the room, her light pink pussy. The room was dark except for a singular bright beam aimed directly at her glistening cunt.

"I don't know," she murmured. No one, not the students, not Grace with the video camera, not Dr. Anderte, seemed to pay her any mind.

"Notice, if you will," Dr. Anderte said confidently, "the changes in tissue color and texture as I perform the exterior exam up and down between the labia majora and the clitoral hood."

Carefully, she pressed a finger into the vulva side groove and worked it along the large lip.

"Perhaps, if two volunteers could assist me . . ." Dr. Anderte looked into the audience. Two women from the front row stepped forward and slipped on latex gloves.

"Yes, thank you." Dr. Anderte stepped back. "If each of you could pull a lip for me. Yes, Alison. Betty, if you could take the other."

Grace stepped aside with the camera as Dr.

Anderte moved to the end of the table between Marla's spread legs.

"I think it would be in everyone's best interest if we formed a circle, close in, around the patient." Dr. Anderte motioned for the other women to circle the examination table. "Fortunately, I have the magnifier and we can take turns observing the next few steps." She reached for the lit magnifier that was attached by a hinged arm to the side of the table and adjusted it between Marla's legs.

The two women with the job of separating the lips leaned to get a better look. Marla felt a slight discomfort as they pulled, almost too roughly, her extended outer lips.

Dr. Anderte tapped the blunt end of the pointer against the clit ridge and circled it gently. "If Alison and Betty would pull the tissue up — yes, that's good — we can observe the full clitoral head. Notice how it juts forward when the skin is stretched back."

Peering into the magnifier, Dr. Anderte dipped the wooden stick into the creamy fluid that had welled between Marla's flappy lower lips. "Ah, yes," she mumbled, tracing the stick's tip from the pussy gel to the exposed clit button. Softly, she painted Marla's white sap against the protruding darkened pearl.

Trying to get a better view of the procedure, the women huddled tightly around the table. The room was quiet except for the heightened sounds of breathing. There were fast-paced panting sounds mingled with deep, almost laborious, longer breaths.

In the center of this tight circle, Marla lay. She

was all too aware of her scent, thick and pungent, simmering in the lamp's direct heat. Sensations of tiny trickles occasionally teased between her legs, and she suspected that welling beads of sweat, laced with her fragrance, were the culprits.

"As you can observe," Dr. Anderte said, momentarily distracting Marla from her self-consciousness, "our patient's clitoris is larger than average."

Dr. Anderte continued to dip her stick into the milky slit and lightly drag it back to the engorged clit bead, tapping against, then circling, the swollen tissue.

"Dr. Anderte," one medical student said hesitantly. Dr. Anderte was always quick to take offense and her students were careful to address her diplomatically. "It's rather difficult for some of us to see exactly what you are . . ."

"Yes, of course," Dr. Anderte said quickly. "Perhaps each of you should have a look in the viewer."

She stepped aside, allowing the first student to peer into the magnifier.

"You will notice the milk-like juice that has accumulated at the vaginal entrance. I would like each of you to dip your gloved finger into the slit so you can feel the consistency."

The first student slipped her finger against the slippery entrance. Dr. Anderte pushed slightly against the student's elbow causing the student's reluctant finger to sink into the opening.

"Don't be afraid to insert deeply. You will see, as you pull your fingers out, that the sex glands lubricate all the way up the vaginal canal."

The student slowly pulled her finger from the heated passage. Marla knew it was probably coated with a white dew.

"Next?" Dr. Anderte motioned for another student. Obediently, the woman ran her finger against Marla's pulsing orifice.

"Try two fingers," Dr. Anderte said, her voice noticeably thicker. "Notice the feel of the vaginal walls as you slide in."

The student pushed her fingers in then pulled them out. Dr. Anderte had her separate her fingers to show the rest of the class how the sex juice spread like spider webbing between her fingers.

Marla lay still as each student had a chance to slip one, sometimes two, fingers into her vagina. Uneasy and embarrassed, she tried to distract herself, to no avail. Consequently her vagina remained tightened by a sustained tension.

After each student had a chance to participate, Dr. Anderte had them return to their seats. Grace, video camera in hand, resumed her position between Marla's legs.

Marla, with the rest of the class, again turned her attention to the monitors. Around the room, a close-up view of her vulva glared at her. Marla was surprised to see how thick, how red it looked. She felt an intense stirring around her clit.

"For sake of a clearer working field," Dr. Anderte said as she pried the smaller lips apart, "I first will cleanse the entire vaginal canal."

She inserted a thick plastic tip into the still creamy orifice. The tip was attached by hose to a large douche bag that hung from a metal rack that Marla hadn't noticed before above the exam table.

Carefully, Dr. Anderte unlatched a valve and water began to spurt from the vagina.

"Marla!" Dr. Anderte exclaimed. "Try to hold the water in as best you can."

Marla tightened her muscles around the thick tip and concentrated on holding the heated liquid inside. Although she found it impossible to retain the fluid, the sensation of fullness, of rushing water, of tightening, created a delicious sensation.

Marla watched the screen as the water seeped, then gushed from her aching slit. She tried to close her muscles completely, but the water continued to defy her.

Dr. Anderte, as though to aid Marla, clamped the slit together with her fingers. Trying to pull the vaginal rim against the thick tip, she pinched the spurting well.

"Oh dear," mumbled Dr. Anderte. She pulled the applicator out and a waterfall rushed between Marla's legs. "Oh dear, oh dear."

As though no longer aware of the rest of the class, Dr. Anderte clamped the valve. Reaching for a towel, she blotted it roughly against Marla's sopping pussy.

"What a waste. What a terrible, terrible waste," Dr. Anderte mumbled frantically. "Have you no retention? Have you no muscle tone?"

Dr. Anderte grabbed a speculum and thrust it into Marla's soaking pussy. Without stopping, she twisted it, turned it, pulled it, pushed it.

"There must be a deficiency. There must be a reason!" Dr. Anderte panted.

Marla watched the metal speculum rapidly push in and out. The tint of her pussy was deep red. The little slit grabbed madly at the hard intruder. Her body was on the edge of explosion. It was just her, just the image on the screen, her red pussy, the fast thrusting, the sopping lips, the creamy slit.

"I don't care, I don't care!" Dr. Anderte tossed the speculum aside and jammed two, then three fingers into Marla. She fucked her repeatedly.

The class was stunned, their eyes riveted to the shocking display on the TV screens. No one spoke, although several seemed involuntarily rocking their legs together.

Marla arched her hips, her legs dropped even further apart. "Dr. Anderte, yes, Dr. Anderte!"

The pounding was relentless. Marla fell into ecstasy while she and the entire class watched her pussy clench hungrily around Dr. Anderte's thick fingers.

Dr. Anderte jerked her fingers out and pressed them against Marla's enlarged clit as if to say, "Yes, I know this kind of pussy, I know what this kind of pussy is capable of." Her fingers whipped across the swollen flesh.

She plunged the douche tip back into the twitching hole and released the valve long enough to allow a short blast of hot water into the tunnel.

Trying to retain the heated liquid, Marla, lost in pleasure, relinquished control. Her muscles relaxed and out gushed the water, whitened by an ejaculation of sex cream. The class watched in awe, Marla watched in awe, as the fluid squirted out from her spasming cunt.

"Oh yes!" Marla screamed. She grabbed the hose tip and pierced it back into her cunt. The water rushed in as she fucked herself, jabbed herself, brought herself to a sopping wet, deliciously hot orgasm.

"Extra credit?" Dr. Anderte contemplated Marla who sat across the desk from her. "It's certainly not my normal protocol."

"I'll do anything to raise my grade," Marla promised. She smiled to herself, reflecting on the fantasy that had just whisked through her mind.

"Yes," Dr. Anderte said dryly. She appraised Marla's suggestive smile. "I suppose you would."

Her Kisses

Last night Elana came over. Last night Elana came over at eleven-fifteen. It was dark, it was cold and it was late. She rode her bike. She rode her bike across town, in the cold, in the dark, because I wanted to sleep with her, because she wanted to sleep with me.

I don't know Elana very well. We've danced at the club, talked on the phone. She's young, twenty-one or some such age that seems distant and unforgivable. Half my age — I could date her mother, be a grandmother to her little infant daughter.

Yet even so, she compels me. We've telephoned each other almost every night this week. Last night, when I called her, I said her name, then waited. I held my breath as she spoke. Her low-pitched voice has a quality that takes me down to childhood. I feel five, maybe six, when she talks. That kind of voice, in a young woman's body, is a volatile mixture.

Her hair is blonde and she paints her lips a crimson hue. She has a butch-boy look but the lipstick casts a distinct femininity to her. I like her looks. I've watched her on the dance floor often. She gets lost in the music. She lets go of her body and she becomes electric light.

Last night after my ex-lover left, I went straight to the phone and called Elana. I felt unsafe, wounded. Something about Elana's voice, Elana's tone, has the capacity to soothe. She seemed to hear my pain, sense my sadness.

"So then tell me," I almost whispered. I wanted her to come over, but I couldn't say the words. I felt too young, too vulnerable. I wanted her to want me. I wanted her to ask me first.

"I want to come over," she said, as though taking the cue. She is so young, yet so aware as if she could read into my silence, could feel me aching.

"On your bike, in the dark, in the cold?" I asked, not really asking at all. I felt unsteady, unsure of what I wanted. My ex-lover was still my lover, but not really. We were not committed, yet we were, but we weren't, but we were. I was weary of entanglements, weary of the pressures of "Now what do we do?"

"You're unsure." Elana's tone was a soft tenor.

"Well, yes, but no." I closed my eyes and imagined her coming through the front door, her face cold from the night, her eyes sparkling and her lips cherry red. "I want you to come."

"Are you sure?" Her voice had a suggestive promise of tenderness.

I was quiet, couldn't speak.

"Yes or no?" she said gently. Her voice was sugar, brandy, melted butter. I envisioned her climbing into my bed. She would be cold from the ride and I would be warm from the blankets. I would cover her, wrap her, take her into my arms.

"Yes, I'm sure," I finally said.

"Good." She hung up the phone.

She was on her way. I visualized her pulling on a sweatshirt, lowering a hat over her short blonde hair. In front of a mirror, she'd paint her lips, blush her soon-to-be-wind-tinted cheeks.

I climbed out of bed and went to my mirror. I smoothed a trail of scent between my breasts, into my hair. We had had several conversations about sleeping together. Both of us wanted the closeness, but were not ready to be sexual. This was what I expected tonight; even so I dabbed on my perfume. I wanted fragrance in my hair when her hands ran through it, when they moved across my back.

I waited, in my bed, writing in my journal about how good it would feel to be held. And she rode in the cold, in the dark, late at night to my house, just to lie in my arms.

Her cheeks were as red as I had imagined and her lips were painted. Her hat, pulled low on her face, made her look even younger. Yet as she climbed into my bed and pulled me into her arms, I felt as if I were much younger than she.

In the darkness, as I lay in her arms, the fragrance that she wore interwove with the scent of the night air. Her hands ran up and down my back, into my hair, across my face. I felt sweet, I felt cherished, I felt protected.

"I just want to feel safe," I whispered. Life had seemed so hard less than an hour ago.

"You are safe," she said.

And her voice was sure and her hands were strong. I wanted to melt into her, to be younger and younger and even younger. I felt as though I were disappearing into her caresses.

"You are so soft." Her voice was velvet.

"Your hands are so strong," I murmured.

My lips brushed her neck. Her skin was smooth, cool against my mouth. Her breath became more noticeable and there was a new determination to her touch. The night light cast a dim glow and I could see her smile as she climbed on top of me. Her mouth was now only inches away. I wanted her, dear God, I wanted her plush lips against mine.

She looked me in the eye, as if to say, "Can I kiss you?" and I turned away. I did not know, I wasn't sure. Her chest was against mine, her heartbeat quick, her breath short. I turned to her.

She pressed her breasts against mine, scissored her legs between mine. Gently running her hands into my hair, she touched her lips to mine.

Her kiss was the sweetest kiss, the only kiss, the

most perfect kiss. Her mouth was moist, heated, and I fell into her, sank into her. I lost myself in the sumptuousness, the suppleness, the remarkably innocent yet sensuous nature of her simple kiss.

I wanted to grab her, to pull her blonde hair, to dig my fingernails into her skin. I was torn between staying in the tenderness and breaking into uncompromising passion.

She did not move. Staying on top of me, she kissed me again, then again. I was soaring in warm softness, in plush heat, in satins and silks. I was hers. Her kiss had opened me and I was lost in its fleshy lushness.

My breathing altered to a pant. My body ached with desire. Her kisses pulled me into a labyrinth of sensual pleasures. Her lips were thick and succulent and as I drank in her moist kisses, I imagined lying between her legs, lapping her sea-salt nectar.

As she sucked from my mouth, I felt the pressure from her hips against my mound. Wanting to give her more room, I spread my legs further. I was damp, the moisture on my panties warm and sticky.

"Elana, you feel so sweet," I whispered.

"Ah, yes." Her words were muffled as she kissed my cheeks, my eyelids, my neck.

I was desperate to have her lips, so seductive, so ripe, back on mine. I framed her face with my hands and guided her to my lips. It was as though my mouth were afire and I needed her moisture to quench the flames.

Her flower-mouth caressed mine and I slid my tongue between the flesh of her sweet lips. Her mouth yielded to me, and my tongue explored the sleek heated tissues inside. I thought of her pussy, of pushing my tongue into that smaller opening. How less giving the interior would be, how the scents, the tastes would differ. I whirled in the fantasy of her delicious mystery and ached to touch, to taste, to bury myself between her legs.

Her arms were tender around me, her mouth open and submissive to my searching tongue. Filled with wild passion, consumed by an urgent heat, I bit into her lip. I wanted to devour her, to smother her, to have every part of her in my mouth.

She let out a small cry. Perhaps I had alarmed her, hurt her with my teeth. I grabbed her, pulled her closer, pressed my mouth harder against hers.

"I want you, all of you," I pleaded, although my words were suffocated by her lips.

She buried her tongue in my mouth, pushed her hands into my hair. Lifting her sweatshirt, pulling at my T-shirt, I arched my breasts to meet hers.

Smooth bodies, soft bodies, we rubbed against each other, still kissing, still engulfed in extraordinary pleasures. Her hips thrust against mine, her breasts teased me, taunted me, then pressed into mine.

I was hers, she was mine. There was nothing but the fragrance of her scent, the silkiness of her skin, the exquisiteness of her sensuous, invading tongue.

Grasping her back, I dug my nails into the vulnerable skin, then slid them into her trousers. Her ass was small and I cupped the round cheeks into my hands. I pulled them apart, grabbed them tightly, shoved her ass till her hips rocked against me again.

Her kisses didn't stop. Her tongue still burrowed, her lips still sucked ravenously on mine.

"I want you, I want you," I mumbled frantically.

But she would not give way. She drank me, absorbed me, swallowed me into her heat, into her slick smoothness. Submerged in her kisses, lost in her kisses, prisoner, slave, whore to her kisses, I gave in. I pulled my hands from her pants and wrapped my arms around her. Never, not for one moment, did my mouth separate from hers.

And we kissed and we kissed and we kissed and we kissed.

Like A Baby

When Mary and Ginny arrived at the town's newest women's bar, the place was packed, the women were hot, and the drinks were cheap. Hoping to find an easy distraction from her recent breakup, Mary drank a quick shot of whiskey and scanned the dance floor.

She had called Ginny in hopes of finding some entertainment for the weekend, anything to get her mind off Evelyn. Mary and Ginny had never spent time with each other. Their prior interactions had revolved around Ginny's group of friends. Mary and

Evelyn would drive into the city from Napa, and Ginny would have the night's events mapped out for the group.

But this weekend, Ginny's lover was away on business and most of her friends were attending a conference so Ginny suggested that Mary join her for dinner and a night on the town.

In the restaurant, Mary had felt a touch of reserve. But as they sipped their wine, the conversation had loosened and Mary's unexpected shyness soon eased to a genuine affability with Ginny.

Ginny had been open, funny, warm. She laughed about her past, talked seriously about her future. She liked her work, hated her boss. Adamant about the need for honesty in a relationship, she felt strongly about commitment and disliked women who cheated. She stuffed herself with desserts, but ate diet food for breakfast. She taped *I Love Lucy, Star Trek,* and *General Hospital,* but otherwise hated TV.

Caught up in Ginny's vibrant personality, Mary's sadness over her recent breakup lifted. Yet when she and Ginny arrived at the bar, Mary sank back into melancholy.

It was the women, so beautiful, so seemingly available, that triggered Mary's low spirits. Nameless, they danced wildly, passed seductive smiles, lifted their jacket collars with intention.

Mary watched, absorbed in fantasies of Evelyn, her ex-lover. With her slick looks and I've-got-what-you-need attitude, Evelyn was probably hanging out in a club, surrounded by women like these, with two, perhaps three on each arm. Evelyn could conquer women with the nod of her head. The thought made Mary nauseous, yet she could think of nothing else.

"I'm at this bar," Mary whispered into Ginny's ear, "with all these hot women, and you want to hear something sick?" She ran her finger over the rim of her shot glass. "All I can think about is how many of these women Evelyn could have. Women are crazy for her, you know. Wherever we'd go, women would look at her, try to make eye contact with her. She's probably on the town right now, without a care, smothered with women." Mary pushed her glass toward the bartender. "Damn, I can't stop obsessing about her."

"Smothered with women, huh?" Ginny motioned for the bartender to refill Mary's glass then casually slid her arm around Mary's waist. "You're going to be okay. I'll see to that."

Mary felt comforted by the friendship Ginny offered. She drank the shot of whiskey, then another, and by the end of the evening, Evelyn's entourage of beautiful women was a swirling dream.

"She can have them all." Mary slurred the words as she slumped into the front seat of Ginny's car.

"She can have the mall?" Ginny said with mock seriousness.

"Yeah, them all," Mary slurred.

Ginny started to laugh and within seconds they slipped into a giggling fit that lasted until they fell into Ginny's bed, exhausted.

"What's the big deal about Evelyn anyway?" Mary mumbled into the darkness.

But the only answer was the sound of Ginny's light snores.

The brightness of the morning sun woke Mary.

At first disoriented, she soon realized that she was cradled in Ginny's arms. Mary shifted slightly and Ginny stirred, her hand drifting across Mary's breast.

Mary lay quietly, listening to the relaxed rhythm of Ginny's breathing. The firmness of Ginny's hand with its slight pressure against Mary's breast aroused her. Mary's heartbeat quickened and her unrestrained nipple tightened.

It had been weeks since Mary had been touched and even the most innocent caress had her body in sudden anarchy. Her nipple refused to relax, her breath slipped into a surprising shallow pant and an insistent wetness welled between her legs.

Although attracted to Ginny's androgynous looks, her wispy short black hair, her steel-blue eyes, Mary was well aware that Ginny *did* have a lover. Over dinner, Ginny had referred negatively to women who cheated. With clear boundaries of her own, Mary certainly wouldn't have sex with a woman under these circumstances. Nonetheless, she was unmercifully aroused.

Mary glanced at Ginny's hand which lightly pressed against her small breast. A rippled gold band decorated Ginny's middle finger and Mary, caught in fantasy, wondered how that band, thick on Ginny's finger, would feel pushed into her wet pussy.

"Ginny?" Mary whispered. "Are you awake?"

Ginny's only response was to slide her hand slightly across Mary's eager breast. Plagued by mixed emotions, Mary knew she should move Ginny's hand. But her nipple, a most willing hostage, protested vehemently.

Ginny's fingers teetered precariously close to

Mary's stubbornly raised nipple, which stiffened, sending a wild aching straight to Mary's hardening clit.

"Ginny?" Mary whispered feebly as she tapped Ginny lightly.

Ginny, apparently deep in sleep, did not respond. Mary waited quietly for a moment, then slid her finger down to her own twitching clit. After all, she thought, there'd be no harm in diplomatically touching herself.

Careful, not wanting to disturb Ginny, Mary pressed her finger along the slippery folds. Wiggling her finger, she gently flicked. Her swollen clit ignited quickly with electric pulsations. Mary increased the light beat, directing her fingertips to her tiny marble-like pleasure center.

It was good, oh yes, it was very good. Even with the lightness and the restricted amount of motion, Mary was able to flutter her clit repeatedly.

Her nipples were knotted, her heartbeat raced. Yes, it was very good indeed. And Mary, who was always unsuccessful at taking herself into orgasm, knew that she was close. Her clit seemed to jump in tiny spasms each time she rubbed it, each time she tapped it lightly.

So close, so very close, but not quite enough — Mary bit her lip, tightened her fist. There was a way, she was certain, to lift herself over that edge, to push through the last block and find absolute, delicious release.

She glanced at Ginny who, seemingly lost in a dream, let out a sigh and shifted slightly. Mary was struck with a red heat as Ginny's hand slid from her breast to her curved waist.

"Ginny?" Mary said meekly. Again, there was no response.

With her fingers still hidden in her honeyed crevice, Mary began to strum her impatient clit. If only, if only, she thought, hungrily eyeing Ginny's thick fingers innocently resting on Mary's rounded belly.

Mary knew what she wanted, knew the very thing that would push her over the edge. Concentrating on Ginny's thick finger, her ridged gold band, Mary increased the pressure against her rigid flesh.

Yes, she thought, imagining those fingers, that band, teasing her wet slit. And to what harm, what harm really, if she were to ease Ginny's hand, slip Ginny's hand, down to the dampness, down to the saturated, engorged flesh?

It was a simple matter of logistics now. As Ginny slept, Mary would borrow — for just a few precious, delicious, luxurious moments — the tips, *and only the tips,* she promised herself — of two of Ginny's fingers. After all, Mary reasoned ravenously, who would know, who would be the wiser?

Mary guided Ginny's unresisting hand between her warm round thighs. Pulling her panties aside, she navigated Ginny's fingers into her sopping wet treasures.

Yes, oh yes, Mary thought, mouthing the words. She was careful not to make a sound, careful not to stir Ginny who slept, undisturbed, at Mary's side.

Mary singled out two of Ginny's fingers and ushered their calloused tips to the swollen edge of her opened slit. Rimming Ginny's roughened fingers around the border, Mary squeezed her own taut desperate nipples, one then the next.

Involuntarily Mary's hips arched and Ginny's fingers, as though they had a mind of their own, entered her creamy warm pussy.

I like it, I like it, Mary thought, or had she actually said the words? She was uncertain. Though it didn't matter, for Ginny slept so sweetly, so soundly, that Mary suspected she could have cried out and it would have gone unnoticed.

Ginny's fingers seemed to pack Mary's cunt — what with their thickness and that showy gold band! Mary tightened as best she could and her pussy grabbed unsparingly at the unsuspecting intruders.

Slowly, she began to grind her pussy. Rotating her hips, she sucked down on Ginny's fingers with her hardened, oil-beaded walls. Yeah, she thought, like that, like that, like that.

Mary pinched her rock-solid clit between her fingers, squeezed it relentlessly as she continued to gyrate on Ginny's fingers. And the ring, with its raised gold waves, rubbed, scratched, almost hurt the sides of her tight cunt. But she didn't care, would never ever care, not the way it scraped her so sweetly.

She grabbed Ginny's wrist and forced the lazy fingers into her dripping heat. Biting into her lip, nearly breaking the skin, she jammed the fingers as deep as she could.

Soaring on those wonderful, powerful, strong fingers, Mary had forgotten about Ginny, had forgotten about boundaries. It was the ring she considered, with its rough texture, the ring she envisioned as it tore at her hardened opening.

She rode the fingers, rocked up and down on the fingers, lost in that momentary madness of pleasure. Her clit felt heavy, as though doubled in size. Her inner muscles clamped unforgivingly.

It had been weeks — seemed like months — since Mary had orgasmed. And as she lifted into the pleasure, she disappeared into a delirious cloud of release.

Mary collapsed, exhilarated. Exhilarated for those few wild moments until she became conscious. And then she remembered. She was in Ginny's bed and it was Ginny's hand. Ginny, whose lover was away. Ginny, who had little regard for women who cheated and no taste for the women they cheated with. It was Ginny's hand, sticky and wet, that was stuffed between her legs.

"Oh God!" She pulled Ginny's hand from her still-throbbing pussy and attempted to blot it on the sheets.

Ginny's body tightened into a small stretch and Mary, whose heart beat frantically, lay quietly for a moment. In a panic, she watched as Ginny went through the motions of waking up. The thought of a humiliating confrontation with Ginny mortified her.

"Gotta pee," Mary mumbled, hurrying from the bed.

"You sleep okay?" Ginny called after her.

Mary leaned against the bathroom wall. Did Ginny's voice have an edge of sarcasm to it, or was Mary, filled with guilt, imagining it? Mary barely remembered what she had actually done, but there was no question it was Ginny's hand she had used. Had she woken Ginny with her brazen sexual episode? Was Ginny angry? Would Ginny tell? The consequences of Mary's foolhardy, sex-driven actions seemed like a monumental gray wall.

"Slept fine," Mary called from the bathroom. She tried to keep her voice calm. "And you?"

"Like a baby," Ginny said lightly.

Trying to keep from laughing, Ginny brought her hand from between the sheets, sniffed the dampness on her sticky fingers and smiled a wicked smile.

43

Married With Kids

I've got a secret, a nasty, nasty secret and there's no one I dare tell. I'm talking breaking rules big time, because the woman I've had my eye on is off limits, way off limits, and I don't care.

She's married, has the big house, the fancy car, three kids and the dog. On the outside her life appears perfect, a fairy tale. But she doesn't fool me, not in the least. Every time we meet, the air is charged. We're static electricity waiting to spark, bottled champagne ready to burst.

When we talk, she stands precariously close as

though naive to the imaginary line she has stepped over. She laughs, shakes her hair, and a breeze of her perfume sweeps me into a mirage of spiced seduction.

Last night, I stopped by her house. When she stepped onto the porch, the brisk winter air urged her nipples into involuntary distention. I tried not to follow my compulsion to stare, but her nipples pushed so tight against her snowy white, thin sweater, that I felt compelled to steal a peek.

Her breasts were small, would fit in my palm, but her nipples were thick and stubby. My desire to run my fingers across the stiff points was brutal and I pushed my hands into my coat pockets.

She played nonchalant, as though neither of us was aware of her rock-hard nipples pouting hungrily against her sweater. She ran her hands through her short black hair, which caused her breasts to jut forward. She acted as if I didn't notice, acted as if she didn't know. But unspoken desire simmered.

My eyes shifted from her freckled nose to her smart-aleck nipples. She continued to flaunt them as she spoke of the kids. Yet she feigned complete innocence, as though unsoliciting my attentions.

During the entire drive home, I thought of her breasts. Her extended nipples, drawn tight, had begged for attention. I imagined pushing her against the door, forcing up her teasing sweater and sucking her darkened tips.

Her husband doesn't like me. The few times he's answered the door, he's barely acknowledged me, no eye contact whatsoever. That's fine with me. I can't stand the jerk. I've got nothing to say to him. It's his wife that's got my fancy.

Last Saturday, she came by my house. Perched on a kitchen stool, she talked about the kids as I cooked dinner. Her skirt was hiked to her knees and I could see the black trim of her stockings. Married with kids and still wearing garters under her skirts, that's my kind of woman.

Her husband doesn't have a clue when it comes to appreciating a woman like her. She's hot, she's itching for some good lovemaking. She wasn't sitting across from hubby with her garters and stockings. She was in my kitchen, on my stool. Crossing and uncrossing her legs, she flashed her cream-colored thighs as she spoke about little Jimmy's report card.

I care about little Jimmy and his report card, but each time she shifted on the kitchen stool, all I could think of was the red lace panties she flashed when she uncrossed her legs.

The shade of her painted lips matched her crimson lingerie. The lipstick, although contrasting strongly her moonlight complexion, was offset by the black beauty mark that teased her lower lip. Her mouth was entrancing. Her eyes, tinted like melted chocolate, intrigued me.

She knows I'm a lesbian. Her husband made that fact very clear from the start, as if that would ensure his wife's subliminal dislike for me. He knew me long before they got together, and believe me, opinions he's got.

But his opinions don't matter to me. What matters is his wife, with her cherry-blossom lips, her shadowy eyes. Contrary to what the husband feels, the wife seems to like me just fine.

I've thought about her all day. She's stopping by tonight with some clothes for me to sort through.

Hubby's taking the kids to a movie and, for the first time, Cathy and I will be completely alone.

I've fantasized this scenario for weeks, time alone with Cathy. No kids, no rush to get home, just the two of us. I've worked on my approach. One wrong move and it's big-time disaster. But, I must admit, a small part of me relishes the risks.

"Hey, anybody home?"

The front door opened and Cathy walked in. I was on the couch, casual like, with the TV on, as though I hadn't heard her knock, as though I had dozed off.

I ran my hands through my hair and shook my head. "Must have fallen asleep," I mumbled.

"Yeah, life of Riley!" Cathy dropped a pile of clothes on the easy chair.

"Two measly days a week," I laughed.

Cathy bent over the clothes and began to separate them. She was talking about the kids but I had trouble concentrating on her words. Instead I focused on her round ass, cupped deliciously by her tight 501s.

Perhaps it was my wishful thinking, but tonight she looked surprisingly like a dyke. With her black boots, jean jacket and checked flannel shirt, she looked like very woman's dream.

"Jerry took the kids to the movies." Cathy turned toward me with a timid smile. Her dark bangs were pushed back from her face by a deep blue bandanna and her almond-shaped eyes were breathtakingly revealed.

"Yeah, you mentioned that earlier." I looked her straight in the eye. There was a lot not being said.

Cathy shifted nervously, haphazardly twisting the buttons on her jacket. "I suppose we've never had any time, just you and me, without the kids or —"

"Or Jerry?" I interrupted. I didn't move from the couch. Instead, holding my ground, I lit a cigarette and inhaled deeply.

She shot me a quick look. "I'm not exactly sure what I'm trying to say . . ."

You're very sure what you're saying, sweetheart, I thought coolly. I took another drag, still watching her fidget in front of me. All my planning, and Cathy was doing the work for me.

". . . but I thought about us being alone together all day."

That was my cue. I ground the cigarette against the ashtray and walked to her. Taking her into my arms, I was instantly mesmerized by her perfume.

"Cathy, I've wanted you," I whispered. I ran my fingertip down the side of her face, across her candy-red lips.

"I'm just not sure . . ."

Oh yes you are, I thought smugly.

"Not sure?" I asked vaguely. I trailed tiny kisses across her smooth cheek.

She was warm, she was soft. I could sense her surrender, her hunger for release. She was clay desperate to be sculpted, harp strings tense with the need to be plucked. I pushed my strong hand around her waist. I was ready to give her just what she wanted.

"What about Jerry?" she said between my kisses.

Jerry, I thought with a sudden anger. He could go fuck himself. As far as I was concerned, his sole purpose was to launch women into lesbianism.

"Shh," I said quickly. I didn't care to hear about Jerry.

I pressed my lips to hers and kissed her, gently. My tongue licked against her mouth and she opened her lips, letting me in. And she kissed me, kissed me as if she had always kissed women, as if she were certain of her direction.

I knew how she felt. Two years before, married with kids, I had given in to a woman's touch. From the very moment that woman had kissed my lips, there had been no doubt where I was headed.

My ex and his new wife had custody of the kids, weekdays. I had weekends, thanks to the asshole judge who thought a straight married couple provided the kids with "stability."

Yeah, straight married couples are real fucking stable, I thought as I unfastened the first button of Cathy's shirt. She didn't protest and I didn't stop. As her shirt fell open, I was seduced by her ivory skin. She was fine china, she was porcelain.

I kissed my way down her neck, inched my mouth against warm skin scented like spring flowers.

"Oh, Cathy, Cathy, Cathy," I whispered as I opened her shirt and exposed her rosy areola.

Her nipple was puckered, thick with desire. I encircled it with my lips and sucked softly on the firm flesh.

"Yes, oh yes," she moaned.

I pulled back from the hard pink tip and opened her shirt completely. As I had envisioned, each small breast boasted a large, ripe nipple.

"I want you. I want you so much." I pressed my face into her fragrant softness. I nestled my face against her breasts. Her stout nipples teased my lips, my cheeks, my eyes. I grabbed her waist, ran my hands up and down her heated back.

My knees weakened and we capsized to the floor. She held onto me, sunk into me, and I moved on top of her. Kissing her, then sucking the plump oversized nipples, I thrust my hips against her. She clamped her legs around my back, held tight as I rode her.

She was mine, there was no turning back. I was starved for her wetness, I ached to slide my fingers, my tongue, my nose into her sweet slickness.

I pulled open her jeans. I was rough, I was fast. I could only think of her sex jelly, I could only think of her white cream. She arched her hips, she was as desperate as I.

Yanking down the jeans, I ripped at her lacy panties and crammed my fingers between her dark-fringed lips. She was wet, she was slippery, she was ready to be fucked.

"Yeah, yeah, yeah," she cried, I demanded. Our words, our thoughts, were interwoven, no longer separate.

Her clit was beefy, out of proportion compared to the small lips. I grabbed it between my fingers and squeezed hard. She was swollen and I milked her unmercifully. Making her thicker, making her heavy, I played her clit like a master. I had her like she had never been had. Clamping the lips wide, I kneaded the chunk of clit flesh. I flicked her, rubbed her, tugged her wildly.

I gave her what she wanted, then teased her till she called my name. She begged me to stop, pleaded for me to continue. She was crazy in her heat, crazy in her lust.

I stretched her wide and slowed my pace, moving my fingertip against her tiny clit tip. She was greased up, like soft butter, and my finger slid easily across the red-capped clit head.

I had her good now. Her clit jutted forward like a sex point and it glistened as I swirled her cunt juice across the erect pod.

Bet she's not thinking of Jerry now! I thought hotly. Bet she could give a flying fuck about him!

"It's so good, so good!" she panted.

"So good, so good," I repeated, still working her.

Yeah yeah yeah, I was greased lightning, I was fucking hot.

I wanted to bring her to climax, show her what sex was really about. As I pumped her hard shaft, I considered my options. I could take her with my fingers. I could take her with my hand.

But what stood out in my mind was my first-rate, sure-fire technique that brought countless women over the edge, unmercifully hard, every time.

I pulled back, taking a moment to watch her squirm.

"Please, please. Oh God, please!" Crying for me to continue, she reached for me desperately.

"Okay, okay, sugar," I said in a soothing tone. "I'll give it to you. Just relax, slow yourself down. Let me take you, my way."

Cathy made a small whimpering sound as she surrendered to my words. Her hands fell to her sides, her body relaxed.

"Good, that's a girl," I whispered.

Gently, slowly, I cradled her clitoris in my mouth, barely touching her flesh. She whimpered again but I didn't move. Skimming the border of her delicate skin with my lips, I teased her until, overwhelmed with her sex-scent, I could hold off no longer.

I pressed hard against her pussy and with the expert skill of a trumpeter, I vibrated my lips. On and on — yes, I had practiced this, yes, I could keep the rhythm forever — on and on — I pulsated, I twittered, I palpated my lips.

She cried, she jerked, erupting in quick spasms of pleasure. Relentless, I fluttered my lips faster. The room filled with an unfaltering humming. I tooted her clit incessantly, playing remarkable riffs, executing a wondrously erotic solo. And Cathy — my deliciously warm, delectably moist, wind instrument — shattered into a symphonic climax.

Sopping wet and utterly satisfied, I collapsed onto her. As she murmured my name over and over, I floated on the aria of her melodic voice.

And the kids, they'd be back with me, where they belong, soon enough. And Jerry, he'd be looking for yet another wife.

The Joy of Cooking

Welcome to the Joy of Cooking

Whether you are a woman who realizes great enjoyment in the kitchen, or whether you are one of the many for whom the idea of even using a spatula seems complicated and overwhelming, this instruction manual is for you.

Success in the kitchen relies on basic principles and techniques. Complete knowledge of kitchenware and accessories is essential to master these culinary skills. The upcoming pages take you on a tour of the cook's basic equipment. Choosing the proper utensil — in size and shape — is important to achieve satisfactory results. In clear, easy steps, each implement, and its various uses, will be explored.

Plunge in and have fun. You and your friends will enjoy the results while you build your new reputation as "terrific in the kitchen."

Selecting Your Kitchenware

It is not necessary for the novice to invest in an array of fancy kitchen accessories. Generally, the basic utensils are already on hand, although often inadvertently shoved to the back of a kitchen drawer and ignored. The full potential of a utensil requires only a good imagination and a willingness to experiment.

If any of the following implements are not already in your kitchen, it is suggested that you make a minimum investment in yourself. Update your kitchen. Once you establish a complete understanding of your utensils and ease of use has been mastered, it is guaranteed that you will utilize each of the items regularly.

Cooking For One

Developing expertise in the kitchen requires practice. Before you attempt to impress your friends with your culinary skills, self-experimentation is recommended. One can try variations on a theme, test what works and what doesn't, gain confidence and perfect technique before scheduling that dinner party. Make your first party "dinner for one." Bring a mirror into the kitchen and treat yourself as the guest of honor. Have fun as you get acquainted with your kitchen utensils.

Household Teaspoon

Even the simplest of tools has a variety of uses. An excellent example is the common teaspoon.

Pre-chill the teaspoon in the refrigerator for a minimum of thirty minutes. Angle your mirror on the kitchen counter so that, when sitting on the counter, you can view yourself completely.

After the spoon has chilled, remove your clothing, climb onto the counter, and angle the mirror so your genital area is in full view. Once accomplished, take the cupped end of the teaspoon and, very lightly, tap the flesh between your lips. Notice the immediate response your tissue has to the cold metal. Has the area tightened? Has it darkened in color?

Continue to tap the different areas of the vulva. Which areas respond? Which areas cause a sensation of arousal? Good cooking relies on complete sensory awareness. Concentrate solely on what you see and how it feels.

Separate the lips and press the spoon directly on the clitoris. A wonderful variation is to rock the spoon back and forth. This, alternated with tapping the spoon along the exterior rim of the vagina, creates a delicious sensation. What a delightful introduction into the personal kitchen experience!

Practice until you have mastered the spoon-tap coupled with the rocking effect. Try your own variations, making mental notes of your different responses.

Tongs

Often, in conjunction with the spoon tap, it is advantageous to use a set of cooking tongs to keep the larger lips separated and out of the working field. Although some prefer to use the tongs at room temperature, many find great satisfaction if they have first pre-chilled the tongs. This is, of course, a personal choice often considered when time is not a factor.

Shimmy the tongs between the lips and separate them as far as possible. The clitoral flange will jut forward and become much more accessible. Tap the smaller end of the chilled spoon against the exposed clitoral head. Note, the head may become temporarily over-sensitive. If this becomes a problem, you may want to consider dampening the areas with a light cooking oil.

Stretch the tongs as far as possible. The vulva skin should be tightened to achieve borderline discomfort. At this point, the first signs of lubrication will become apparent at the mouth of the vagina. Carefully dip the teaspoon into the entrance and scoop a small amount of the cream. You may want to sample the taste. Please keep in mind that if you do taste, this flavor will become more concentrated as the lubrication wells.

Honey Dipper

Although unfairly labeled with the confining name "honey dipper," this utensil is actually multi-faceted in its usage. Whether wooden or plastic, this simple tool has become an integral part of the kitchen connoisseur's repertoire.

Using your forefinger, twirl your seeping lubrication, or if needed, cooking oil, around the mouth of your vagina. When sufficiently moistened, press the honey dipper against the opening. Surprisingly, you may find it difficult to press the dipper into the vaginal cavity. Many beginners stop at this point, unclear how to proceed. A true understanding of the honey dipper's interesting shape is necessary to have success with insertion of this remarkable tool.

Because the honey dipper, in shape alone, is a distant cousin to the wood screw, the technique for insertion is similar to that of the screw family. The unhurried, methodical approach — slowly twisting the head of the dipper, carefully applying pressure, is the most popular.

Begin with a gentle turn. As you watch in the mirror, you should note the mouth of the vagina as it slowly swallows the thick head of the dipper. With each rotation, the dipper will inch deeper into the flesh. Pay attention to the internal pressure as the honey dipper twists along the interior walls. Has this sensation caused your clitoris to thicken further? Have the smaller lips tightened or expanded? Has the clitoral head poked out from the hood? Is the color pink, red or purplish?

Using continual inward and outward corkscrewing motions, tease the bulb of the honey dipper deeper with each inward stroke until desired insertion depth is established.

Another technique often used is the combination dipper-tong approach. Once the dipper is halfway inserted, stretch the outer vulva flaps apart with the tongs. Tap the spoon along the clitoral ridge simultaneously. This creates a multi-erotic sensation that is hailed among experts in the culinary field. But remember, this step takes practice, practice, practice. Don't get frustrated with the difficulty of the combined techniques. The more you try, the easier this becomes.

The Baster Family

Of the many basting options, the two most popular are the stiff brush baster and the bulb baster. Although these basters can be used independently of each other, the combination concept, which will be discussed here, is considered standard.

The brush baster is similar in appearance to a miniature broom. The brush portion is unyielding in texture, but when used with a condiment, such as honey or oil, the bristles become more flexible.

The brush baster often is used to apply, or paint, the entire vulva area. Dipping the brush into warm honey, for example, and slathering the glaze onto the clitoral pouch, is one way to increase stimulation and arousal in this area. Slow, strong strokes, with considerable pressure, are recommended.

As the brush glosses the flesh, consider once again stretching the lips apart. Observe the changes in the clitoral bead itself. Often, the clitoris will protrude dramatically. It is not unusual to notice a direct change in coloration of the rim of vaginal flesh. Is there a throbbing sensation at the border rim of your vagina?

An interesting addition to this technique is to include the bulb "turkey" baster. Having already filled the plastic tube with warm water, place the tip above the vaginal entrance. As you continue to apply the honey in long, well-defined strokes with the brush baster, aim the bulb tip against the clitoral hood. Alternate between squirting, then sucking, the heated water.

Does the flushing sensation cause the clitoris to ache? Does the continual spurting of water on its delicate head create a grasping sensation in the vagina?

Meat Baller

One of the most misunderstood of the kitchen utensils is the lone meat baller. With its scissor-like handles on one end and the large circular cups on the other, most tend to ignore this tool, never to consider the options it offers.

Simply stated, using the meat baller to tug the nipple area, creates an unrivaled arena of sensation. A word to the impatient — it is not unusual to have difficulty fine-tuning the correct pressure for clamping the nipple, considering the baller's bulky metal cups. But once in place, the resulting effect is well worth the patience and effort you invest.

Keep the ball halves slightly apart for grasping purposes. Carefully slide the areola flesh between the cups. Slowly close the halves, seizing the base of the nipple shaft, until a light tension is generated. Applying additional pressure, wiggle the nipple pellet. Twist, turn, then pull. Twist, turn, then pull until you have scraped the metal ball along the entire length of the nipple.

For added effect, squeeze one nipple between your thumb and forefinger while simultaneously clamping the other nipple with the meat baller. A favorite of many epicureans is to shift the barely opened cups in a small counter-clockwise direction. Take your time, experiment. Do you feel the cups press the sensitive nipple as you rotate the baller? Is the sensation stronger with the ball halves clenched together? If you tug the handles does an insistent tingling occur in your clitoral region?

The Electric Mixer

This last technique is recommended for the experienced kitchen worker, but is included to motivate the novice to reach beyond her goals.

Cover the entire vulva area with a thick pot holder. Although this will limit the visual possibilities, the tactile sensations will more than make up for the sacrifice.

Place the electric mixer's beaters against the pot holder. Holding the pot holder firmly in place, turn the mixer on to low speed. As the vibrations build, continue to increase the speed. **Do not let go of the pot holder.**

Does the beating of the mixer cause involuntary contractions in your vagina? Are the sensations you are experiencing reaching orgasmic level?

From Novice To Expert

Let experience be your guide. Your personal timetable depends on your knowledge of the utensils and the skills you have developed. Take your time and relax. Before long, you'll be an expert and your confidence will soar.

With your self-confidence bolstered, take the next step, plan that dinner party! Soon enough, you'll find that dinner guests really will mean it when they ask, "How can I help?"

Today's novice is tomorrow's "whiz in the kitchen." Enter the world of culinary delights, come to the joy of cooking.

Sex With Allie

Allie wants me. The spark in her eyes when she said my name, the cockiness of her walk as she entered my house, the curl of her upper lip when she smoked her Camel, it was written all over her.

She's only been back in town two weeks, but I can feel it all the same. Allie's no fool. She knows how to play a situation. She wants me and she's taking her time.

Sex with Allie intoxicates, seduces. Like a few shots of tequila or a couple hits of weed, sex with Allie is my jones, my addiction, my dead-end street.

"I want to come see you," she said on the phone. And my stomach dropped like a rush down a roller coaster track. My mind argued, *Don't let her come,* but somehow the words never reached my mouth.

Allie makes statements with her choice of clothing. It's her trademark. When I opened the door, Allie — in a black leather jacket unzipped to the lace of her black bra, her tight black jeans framing her curved hips — was clearly stating that she wanted me.

"Hello, Erica." Her voice was heated and I thought of the warmth of her skin.

When she hugged me, her arms took me in, reminding me how tightly she has grasped me during pleasure. Her scent, her soft breasts, her hard nipples, I envisioned it all.

As though she never left, Allie sauntered in. She has that way about her, an innate ability to negate all the hurt she causes with a simple hug. I hate that about her. I love that about her.

She propped her feet on the coffee table, like she used to do, and ran her hands incessantly through her ginger-brown hair as she spoke. I'm certain she wore the pointed black boots deliberately because the last time she made love to me, she was wearing them. That's Allie's style all right, conjuring up old images to get new results.

I'm no fool. Allie thinks, just because she wants me, just because she flaunts her sun-bronzed cleavage beneath her black leather jacket, above her black lace bra, that I'm going to fall into bed with her.

Well, I've walked that road too many times. She

can tempt me all she wants. All to no avail, I can tell you that.

Allie brought me a bottle of Shalimar perfume. She got it, duty free, in Paris. She says she saw the perfume and thought of me. That's Allie for you, always playing the angles.

The bottle of wine Allie brought was French and we sipped it as she talked about Paris. She sets up atmosphere, like the way she chooses her clothes, with intent.

She spoke of her trip and occasionally, a French word would slip in, as if by accident. As she talked, I had a vivid recollection of her hands pushing at my body, pressing into my breasts as she'd whisper *"Je tu desire."*

Since Paris, Allie's become quite the femme. Dark pink lipstick shimmered on her plush lips. Her mahogany eyes were shadowed in green-silver tints. And her sable hair, which was longer, fell seductively over her eye.

Her gaze never drifted from me, or so it seemed. Allie can do that, even from a different room. Her eyes pierce like she has a power to burn through walls. Even when I went to the bathroom, I sensed her watching and kept the lights off.

When Allie left, she kissed me lightly on the lips and left a pink stain on my mouth. I know this because I looked in the mirror after the door had closed, just to see the imprint of her mouth on my own.

The room was filled with Allie's scent. She said her cologne was a new fragrance she had bought in France, but it smelled unforgivingly like Georgio for

Men, the cologne she used to wear when we were lovers. Her scent was everywhere, and I suspected that she had somehow sprayed the room before leaving. She likes to do that sort of thing, ease her way in subtly. Not this time, not with me.

Allie's wine glass flaunted a pink lip print on the rim. I brought her glass to my mouth and sipped the last drops of wine. My tongue lightly grazed the rough area from the lipstick and I licked it carefully.

Allie has a sensuous mouth, a ravishing mouth. Her tongue is warm velvet and her lips are coral rosebuds. Her mouth is luscious as it suckles, as it pleases. Slow and easy, her kisses adore. Fast and crazed, her kisses possess.

Before France, before she left me, I remember how Allie had loved me with her mouth. Running her tongue across my nipples, she slowly circled one, then the other. My nipples pushed up from the wrinkled areolas as though in desperation. She sucked one into her mouth and created a hard suction. With her fingers, she twisted the other nipple, tightly stretching the pink stub as far as she could. When she'd let go, the erect tissue perched hungrily from my breast.

Slowly moving her lips down my belly, Allie traced the fringe of the black hair that grew full on my pussy. I knew that her tongue was inching toward my dampness and I spread my legs in anticipation.

Allie spread my lips with her fingers and tapped her tongue the entire length of my pussy. She spread me so far, I could see the pink flesh rise between her fingers. Her tongue dabbed lightly across the shaft and I lifted my legs to her shoulders.

"I love that," Allie said.

And she does. When I put my legs on her shoulders she gets crazy. She pushed my knees further apart and burrowed into my sopping wet folds.

Allie lapped her tongue across my pussy and repeatedly lashed my clit ridge. I could feel her right on my spot and told her over and over how good it felt.

Allie looked up, her face glazed with my juice that glossed her like liquid sugar. She looked me straight in the eye, with those penetrating eyes, those eyes that can see through walls, and said, "I want to see more."

"Anything, anything," I moaned as I spread myself apart for her. I wanted her to see every crease, every fold, every hardened tissue.

"No," Allie murmured. "What I want is this." She reached into her jacket and pulled out a leather pouch. "I want to see all of you."

She went into the kitchen and returned with a bowl that steamed slightly. I sat, as though in a stupor, and watched her pull silver scissors from the bag.

"You trust me, don't you?" she said hypnotically.

Silver flashed as she lifted them. Gently she rested the point against my pubic hair.

"Can I trim you? Can I wear your hair in a locket?"

Allie ran the point along the edge of the hair. I felt a light scratching along my skin. So she wanted to wear my hair in a locket. So she said. But I knew Allie. She was transient, here for the moment and nothing else. Yet when Allie made love to me, what she wanted was all that mattered, even if she walked out and never came back.

I nodded and Allie smiled her dazzling smile. "Wait till you see how pretty you will be," she promised.

She began to trim, carefully, until the dark hair was flat against my skin. She pulled a small mirror from the pouch. "See?" She positioned the mirror between my legs. "See how pretty?"

I could see my trimmed pussy in the mirror. My clitoris poked between the nearly hairless lips, and the smaller lips were remarkably visible.

"And now," Allie said ceremoniously. "For the grand finale!" She pulled an ornate, silver razor from the pouch.

"Allie, I don't think —"

I tried to protest, but was distracted by the sweet sensation of her full lips suckling my clit. She nursed me like a baby would a large nipple and she inserted several fingers into my pussy. Slowly she pulled her fingers in and out, in and out as she flattened my clit between her lips.

"Let me, baby, let me make you my little girl."

Her fingers pried in, then out. Her tongue flicked my heavy clit. Over and over, she begged for her pleasure.

"Let me make you mine, let me lather you up and turn you into my little girl."

"Okay, yes, okay," I panted. Allie had me hot. I'd do anything for Allie.

Allie dipped her fingers in the bowl and dribbled

a warm liquid onto the light layer of hair. She rubbed the dampness gently and it lathered into creamy bubbles.

She edged the razor against my skin. "My little girl," she whispered.

Slowly, carefully, like an exacting artist, Allie scraped the sharp blade against the remaining hair. When there was no more hair above my pussy, she looked up and smiled.

"And now for those dark thick lips." She pulled my pussy lip taut and tilted the razor against the fragile skin.

"Allie, not there." I grabbed her hand.

"Shouldn't grab a hand with a razor," Allie said nonchalantly. She paused. "I'll stop if you want."

I glanced at my pussy. Allie still had the lip pulled tight and my clit throbbed from the tension. Sensing my passion, Allie slid the blunt end of the razor handle against the bead tip of my clit and swirled it lightly.

My clit felt inflamed. The rough tip of the razor's handle scratched yet thrilled my hot cunt. She pulled the lip further.

"Let me smooth you down, baby."

The razor handle pressed and prodded against my tiny core. Rough like a calloused finger, like a kitten's tongue, like a nail file, it stimulated me unmercifully.

"Let me smooth you down, baby," she whispered again.

And of course, I spread my legs further in hopes of letting Allie all the way in.

She stretched the lip so tight I let out a cry. It hurt, yet it pleased me in an unnatural way. The blade grazed the tender flesh repeatedly until the lip was chafed and hairless.

"And the other," Allie said seductively, again circling my clit with the razor's handle.

She grabbed the other lip, almost pinching the skin between her fingers, and extended it from the clit shaft. My entire sex area was beet red and willingly took any attention it could get.

Deftly, she ran the razor blade across the lip, removing the remaining hair in quick short strokes.

"I like your pussy bare, I like it red and raw," she said, her voice thick.

"Yes, me too, me too." I wanted her to take my clean-shaven pussy and slam it good.

"Yeah, yeah, yeah," Allie muttered. She spilled more liquid on me and lathered me further. In the creases, in the folds, she washed me, fast, vigorously. "Yeah, yeah, yeah."

Her strong fingers, with their intentional beat, their remarkable rhythm, drummed insistently between my fleshy exposed lips.

"Oh, Allie. Yes, Allie. Please, Allie," I moaned. I grabbed her hair and tugged her toward me.

Allie pressed her face against my breasts. With quick, sharp bites, she pinched the tender flesh around my nipples. Her nails pushed into my back, scraped me. It hurt, it felt good. She was too rough, not rough enough.

I twisted my fingers into her hair and jerked her mouth from my stinging nipples. Her face was wild. Her eyes were copper lightning, her mouth was pink fire.

Allie took over. She pushed the coffee table aside

and pulled us both onto the floor — she on the bottom, me on the top.

"Straddle me," she pleaded. "Let me see my artistry."

I knew Allie and what she wanted. I squatted so that my newly shaved, red pussy was suspended over her face.

"Is this what you want?" I opened the lips with my fingers and dangled my swollen flesh precariously close, deliciously close, teasingly close to her anticipating, outstretched tongue.

"Jesus, you are fucking beautiful," she muttered.

I was wide open, completely exposed, as I bobbed the full bulb of my clitoris inches from her lapping mouth. I pulled my chafed lips even further apart and was afforded a view of my bloated clit flesh.

The flash of my pinkness, bulky and inflated, sent a rush of desperation through me. An uncompromising ache throbbed on the skirting ridge of my opening.

"Allie, please," I begged.

Allie, long before, had found a spot on the entrance of my vagina that, when worked just right, pushed me into splintering pleasure. Only Allie, with her determined fingers, her urgent fingers, could find what she called my "velvet."

"Give up the velvet," she whispered.

Still in a squatting position, I spread my legs further. When my legs were spread, when I squatted low, it caused the thick tissue just inside my slit to protrude. Allie had taught me this, had had me squat over countless mirrors while she trailed her fingertips on the inner flesh. This was when she could find my velvet spot. This was when, with the smallest of circular motions, she could drive me wild.

I squatted, my legs spread, the tension on my inner thighs hard. She rested her tongue on the side of my clit as she wiggled her finger against the distended inner flange of pussy.

Slowly, she slid her tongue down the side of the clitoral ridge and held it close, but not on, my pounding clit head.

"C'mon, c'mon," I begged.

My pussy was wide, my pussy was ready. One tap, one circle with her fingers and I would blow.

She rimmed my velvet, she teased my velvet. I cried out as if in pain. "C'mon, c'mon!"

Allie knew me, all right. It's just like Allie to wait until that last moment, until I couldn't take anymore.

Allie flicked her fingers against the spot, circled her fingers across the spot, pressed her fingers along the spot as she sucked my hard clit into her mouth.

I screamed and a delirious pleasure surged through me. Allie was the one. Only Allie can take me to that place, and she knows it.

That's Allie for you. She's got that kind of charisma. If you let her get started, she'll bore her way in, seduce you with pleasure, get a hold over you like no one else, then walk out your door — maybe for a day, maybe for a month, maybe forever.

When Allie showed up at my house today, it was written all over her face. She wants me. She's trying to sweet talk her way back into my pants with

French wine and perfume, wants to remind me of our past passion with black boots and Georgio for Men. That's Allie for you, all right. And tonight, when she comes back, I'm going to do my best to tell her no. I'm no fool.

Happy Birthday, Baby

On the cutting edge of her life, tonight, at eight-forty-two, Frances Larson turned forty. Her celebration was simple, for it wasn't the actual date that held significance for her, it was the idea. What intrigued her was the launch into a new decade, the thrill of this up-and-coming era.

She had long suspected that her forties would be her time. Even during the last few weeks, almost as a prelude, she had noticed subtle changes within herself. She felt a sense of calm, a new comfortableness with herself. The drama of her past relationships was finally being laid to rest.

In her own way, Frances decided to have a party. She bought a bottle of Moet champagne, a flowered tin of bath salts, a plush satin dressing gown and a bottle of Picasso perfume. She spent a small fortune, but forty was forty.

Tonight her bedroom glowed in a canopy of light. Frances had unwrapped the antique candelabra her grandmother had sent and adorned it with sixteen tapered candles.

Relishing the lusciousness of her satin robe, Frances listened as water filled the tub. The floral scent from the bath salts drifted lazily into her bedroom.

"Happy Birthday, baby," she whispered as she caressed the smoothness of her robe.

Her hands slid slowly against the rich material draped around her waist. She had the body of a woman who had seen time pass, the curves of a woman who had let life push through it. She had nursed her babies, had sat for countless hours as they suckled her sweetened milk, and now her breasts hung softly, her hips blossomed from her rounded belly.

She did not regret her softness, did not regret the loss of the ideal, for her body was plush, well-ripened. She had the body of a woman who was not afraid of life.

Frances let the robe fall. The water steamed into a fragrant mist that wrapped her in a sultry warmth.

She dipped a foot into the water which was almost too hot. Slowly, she squatted into the heat, then submerged the entirety of her sex which ached in hot pleasure.

Within moments her body befriended the heat, and Frances was consumed with a honey-sweet tranquility. She floated in steamy dreams, lingered in misted clouds. The perfume from the salts tantalized her senses. She was in a floral field, a musky forest, a tropical garden.

"Get out of the tub, birthday girl," a voice murmured in her dream.

Frances drifted in the melody of the words which coaxed her further into the haze.

"Get out of the tub, birthday girl," the voice purred hypnotically.

There was movement, then everything was black. A soft blindfold had been pushed in front of Frances's eyes.

"What —" Frances said in mock protest, for she recognized the voice, knew exactly who had covered her eyes. It was her best friend Brooke.

"That's right, birthday girl," Brooke said as she guided Frances out of the water. "We've brought you your birthday present."

The sudden coolness of the air caused Frances's nipples to tighten into hard buds. She shivered, partly from the cold, partly from anticipation.

"Here," a deeper voice mumbled.

A towel was wrapped carelessly around Frances. The blindfold was tightened around her eyes and she was led out of the bathroom.

"Do you know who's with me, birthday girl?" Brooke said teasingly. She led Frances to the edge of the bed. "Give the birthday girl a hint."

"Hello, Frances."

It was Joyce, Frances was certain of that. She envisioned Joyce's titian hair and ice-blue eyes and recalled their power to hypnotize. Joyce was Frances's confidante. They had gossiped over countless cups of coffee, seen every new movie together, laughed late into the night.

"We're partners." Brooke pressed Frances onto the bed. Her lips grazed Frances's ear as she spoke, her straight black hair fell across Frances's face.

"In the perfect crime," Joyce added. Her words had a subtle bite to them as she spread Frances's legs apart.

Frances felt suddenly disoriented. Brooke and Joyce were crossing strict boundaries. Brooke had long ago insisted that friendships were best left platonic, even though Frances had, on occasion, admitted a secret desire to feel Brooke's long, butch fingers swirl in her wetness. But at Brooke's request, Frances had learned to keep her desires captive to nighttime fantasies.

Joyce also had made it clear that she didn't want to risk their friendship for, as she said, "a momentary taste of the sweet." So Frances had left well enough alone.

As Frances was being led by her two best friends — perhaps the two hottest women she knew — into the bedroom, she felt dizzy with the possibilities. It seemed that Brooke and Joyce had planned a surprise party of their own.

"Brooke wants to know how you like to be fucked, don't you, Brooke?" Joyce said dryly.

"As a matter of fact," Brooke said sarcastically, "it would be nice to *see* rather than hear, the details of her torrid encounters."

"I couldn't agree more, Brooke," Joyce said as she teased the full thatch of hair between Frances's legs.

"So, I want to see how you like getting fucked," Brooke said again. She lightly kissed Frances's mouth. "Would you let Joyce do that for me, sweetie?"

Acutely aware that she wore only a blindfold and a towel, Frances nodded. This was a fantasy come true. Never, in her wildest dreams, had Frances considered a ménage à trois with her best friends. Not only had Brooke and Joyce made it individually clear that sex with Frances was off-limits but Joyce and Brooke barely liked each other.

Now Brooke wanted to watch how Frances liked to be fucked. Spiraling with heat, Frances spread her legs and arched. She hoped to temp Joyce into opening her pussy further.

"Not so fast," Joyce said roughly.

"That's the problem with Frances," Brooke said quickly. "Always tries to control things. But you're not the host of this party, are you, Frances?" She pushed Frances's arched body back to the bed.

"I suppose not," Frances whispered.

"You supposed right." Joyce then said to Brooke, "Hold her arms down."

Brooke clasped Frances's hands together above Frances's head. "Like this?"

"Perfect." Joyce pulled the towel from Frances. "You do want her to hold your arms down for me, don't you, Frances?"

"Yes," Frances moaned. She was swept into exhilaration. She imagined how Joyce's strong biceps would flex, she imagined Brooke's long fingers lightly flicking her clit. Both of her friends, thick fingered partners, were preparing to work on her. "Yes, hold me down. Please hold me down."

Joyce gave Brooke a slick smile. Although Joyce respected Brooke, she never figured what Frances saw in her. She secretly thought Brooke's overdone "butch appeal" was overkill. As far as Joyce was concerned, she'd show Brooke a thing or two about how a true butch worked a woman, no question about that.

Joyce carefully peeled back the thick lips that covered Frances's red sex like a matted blanket. The flesh glimmered in the candlelight.

"That's very nice," Brooke said as she watched Joyce's maneuvering.

The clit, perched on a pedestal of voluptuous folds, poked dramatically from Frances's nest of hair.

"Ample," Joyce said. "Frances has an ample pussy." She stretched the pussy lips so that the clit jutted as though it would droop from heaviness if Frances were to stand.

"I've always liked big clits," Brooke added. She ran one of her hands across Frances's nipples that stood up like oversized, rouged kernels.

Joyce pressed the meat between her thumb and forefinger and pushed the abundant tissue aside.

"Take a look at her clit head," Joyce said as she continued her strokes. "It's the size of a pea."

"Let me see." Brooke shifted to get a better look.

Joyce stretched the pulp back from the clit tip to expose its hard pink helmet.

Holding Frances's wrists with one hand, Brooke licked the tip of her finger and glazed the blushing-pink bud with her saliva. A shiny film laced the flamboyant bead. Easily, dreamily, she circled the clit then nudged the little shaft with her fingers.

Frances suddenly arched, as if she wanted Brooke to play her pussy, as if she wanted Brooke's touch, as if, from the circling pressure, Brooke could drive her into hard climaxes. Joyce suspected that in Frances's fantasies, Brooke had done it countless times. Well, she'd show Brooke.

"Come on baby," Frances pleaded. "You know how I like it."

"She says you know how she likes it, Brooke." Joyce pulled her fingers from Frances's wetness. The pussy folds covered the head as they thickened back against Brooke's flicking finger.

"Yeah, but I thought I was going to watch you fuck her," Brooke replied, still massaging the erect clit as she spoke.

Joyce pushed two fingertips against Frances's gaping rimmed slit. A milky cream had seeped from the portal and Joyce swirled her fingers in the oily crease.

Frances gaped. Her body, still arched, danced in small, anxious, jerking motions.

Frances was immersed in pleasure. Feeling Brooke's fingers zero in on her clit, she clamped her sex muscles tight. C'mon, c'mon, Joyce, she thought desperately. Fuck me hard, fuck me hard.

Brooke played Frances's clit. The reddened tissue had ballooned, doubling its size, and she had to silently concede that she had never seen a woman's clit so thick and large. Joyce continued to pound her fingers deep into Frances as if to show her how hard she could fuck, how fast.

In response, Brooke dribbled her finger back and forth over Frances's pleated clit. She had Frances hot, no doubt, there was sex cream all over her fingers. She had never seen a vulva so exaggerated in size. She watched how fast, how hard Joyce moved inside Frances. Joyce plowed into Frances at a nonstop pace.

Brooke increased her flicking, twiddling the entire clit between her fingers. She pinched it easily, she pulled it as though expressing milk from a cow's teat.

And Frances, who had probably never felt her cunt so hard, so heavy, shot off into an intense, long, body-stuttering come. She arched, she jerked, her body convulsed in desperate ecstasy.

So there, Brooke thought as she glared at Joyce.

Joyce gave Brooke a hard look.

"Turn her over," Brooke demanded quickly, flashing Joyce a "teamwork" smile. "Come on, let's get a look at her pretty ass."

Frances no longer could decipher who was who. Hands pushed her, hands rolled her, hands forced her onto her stomach. Prying hands, demanding hands rushed up her back, down her buttocks.

She moaned as she arched her body. "Yes, yes."

"Spread her apart. Spread her apart for me."

The hands separated the full mounds of Frances's ass. Frances imagined how she looked with her rounded ass pulled apart, exposed for both Joyce and Brooke. She filled with a mixture of vulnerability and extreme sexual desire and lifted her ass higher.

Fingers pried her, sank into her wetness. Her ass cheeks were stretched and a finger boldly teased the tight, but slowly relaxing orifice.

"Fuck her in the ass."

"Do you want it in the ass, birthday girl?"

The finger pushed against the tiny bud opening, first lighty, then with a demanding urgency. Frances felt a rush of cold lube soak her tender slit.

"Yes, yes, yes," Frances cried. She tried to lunge against the thick finger as it swirled the gel.

With a quick thrust, the finger pressed into the secret orifice. Simultaneously, two fingers jammed into her aching, larger slit. Another rode her clit. There was movement, furious movement, as all the fingers shot into her, played her, slammed her, took her. And Frances, like never before, screamed her passion as she released climax after climax.

The hands stopped and Frances collapsed onto the bed. The room filled with a smoldering silence. Brooke pulled Frances up and led her to the bath. The water was still warm as she guided her back into the tub and removed her blindfold.

"Happy birthday, baby." Brooke kissed Frances lightly on the cheek.

"Yeah, happy birthday," Joyce said.

* * * * *

Frances watched as her not-so-compatible friends exchanged hot butch smiles. Filled with luxurious contentment, she closed her eyes. Yes, she was very much looking forward to her forties.

Out-of-Town Girl

She says she spotted me first, but from across the room I'd already felt her eyes burn into me. I was a dressed down, casual, out-of-town girl just blending in, yet her eyes zeroed right in.

It's uncommon for women to approach me. My buddies say my "high-powered" femme image intimidates most butches, a social phenomenon I've learned to accept. But on those rare occasions when a self-confident woman makes her move, I get weak in the knees.

I'm always an easy girl when a butch woman

comes on to me. It's that simple. Looks can be deceiving. I may appear cool, hard to get, but when I'm approached first, I'm an easy, easy girl.

She sent me a smile from across the bar. Her eyes suggested a stirring interest. I smiled shyly, then glanced toward the pool table — number five sliced into the corner pocket. Yes, I thought, returning a smile, I'm interested, too.

The cue ball flirted with seven but led her astray, and the woman moved, like a smooth shot, to my side.

"Can I buy you a drink?"

Her eyes were dark as starless nights and her summer-petal lips bloomed full. Her coal-colored hair, tightly woven into a short braid, was a backdrop to her ginger-tinted skin. An island woman.

"Sex on the beach," I replied with a seductive smile.

"Excuse me?"

How long I had waited for this moment, to ask for this drink, simply to say its name. I'm not a drinker, had no idea what was in it, but the words, *sex on the beach,* had their implications. The woman blushed.

When a butch woman blushes, she crosses a subtle boundary. Momentarily out of control, she lets go. It's like orgasm. When I make a butch woman blush, it's almost as sweet as making her come.

"Sex on the beach? Is that a drink or a suggestion?" She laughed.

Her eyes locked into mine then drifted to my breasts where they brazenly lingered. I felt heat simmer between my legs as she appraised what I had to offer. Out-of-towner, easy girl, seated on a bar stool, waiting for my drink.

The drink burned sweet as I sipped it slowly. Discreetly, I watched her walk toward her friends. The pool table stretched between us like a worn forest floor and the cue ball escorted the eight ball to the corner pocket.

"Yes!" shouted the winner. Her right hand pushed into the air in a signal of victory.

The butch woman flashed me a hot smile, then slapped the winner on the ass.

"Good job, Terry."

"Yeah!"

A small, dark woman placed the balls on the table, rounding them up into a triangular corral. The women shifted.

My butch woman cornered the pin ball machine. I had a compelling urge to walk to her, stand by her, root for her as she challenged the machine. But my eyes returned to the tabled corral. I had a straight-line relationship back home. Accepting the drink was a harmless splintering of that line, but a walk to the woman would form a definite triangle.

I took several quick sips of my drink. The warm haze from the liquor slid through me then nudged my inhibitions. My thoughts were pleasantly blurred and the geometrical considerations suddenly seemed less definitive. The walk to the woman was appearing less like a triangle and more like an arrow.

Nah, I thought with a light-hearted giggle. Maybe a diamond? Maybe a star?

The DJ tempted me with a pulsating song and I

drifted to the dance floor. The music swept through me like the heat from my drink and I swayed hypnotically to the music. I glanced to my island woman who smiled then walked toward me and asked me to dance.

A slow dance and she held me with intention, held me like a lover, held me like she, and no one else, belonged in my arms. I pressed into her, floated into the alluring scent of her cologne. Drakkar. I knew the scent. A tourist, out-of-towner — tomorrow I would go to the shops and spray my island woman's scent onto my wrist. This I knew about myself, how I handled my fantasies.

"Take you home?" she whispered in my ear.

"Ride with a stranger?" I murmured. After all, she was indeed a stranger. Never ride with strangers, never take their candy — the voice of my mother still haunted me thirty years later. "Do you also offer candy?"

I had an impulsive urge to flirt with danger. *Out-of-town girl climbs in car with butch stranger and disappears* — tomorrow's headlines didn't faze me. At that moment, to the out-of-town, girlfriend-back-home-treating-me-like-I'm-nothing girl, those headlines seemed like good news.

"Don't worry, I'm a cop." Her tone blended reassurance with provocation.

In my arms, a butchwoman with a police badge was offering to take me home. I had a sudden fantasy of leaning over her car, legs spread, as she searched for illegal contraband. Then I wouldn't be stepping out on my girlfriend back home. Then it wouldn't be cheating. I'd simply be a tourist, wrongly accused, victim of a local, bully island cop. I hoped I looked suspicious.

She drove a Harley adorned with polished chrome, and we rode into the warm, island night. From the hills, she showed me the Waikiki lights. From the beach she offered the restless ocean.

"Should I take you home?" she asked, her voice cool as the night air had become.

"Yes, I suppose that would be the best," I said vaguely. I didn't want to go back to the hotel but the brisk air had had a sobering effect and the hope of a police search was a fading fantasy.

Communication, by itself, can be a wondrous thing. She took me home all right, her home. What harm? We climbed off the bike wordlessly.

"Damn," she said as she jiggled the front door handle. "I thought I left this unlocked."

"No key?" I asked, let down. The one time the fantasy was worth a step out of my relationship and here we were locked out.

"No big deal," she said with a peppery smile. "You got a credit card?"

"Well, I suppose . . ." I pulled one from my back pocket.

"That's the beauty of these old houses," she said matter-of-factly as she pried the lock with the card. "Three jiggles and the locksmith loses his job."

A stained-glass lamp lit the small living room, otherwise the house was dark.

"Have a seat." She motioned to an overstuffed couch. "There's one last part of Hawaii I think you should experience."

Her eyes enticed as she pulled a small ivory box

from her jacket. "This is Hawaii's gold," she said, her words shrouded in sudden mystery.

The room filled with an exotic fragrance of freshly mowed fields and plush tropical forests. She crumbled a bud of green-gold leaves between her fingers and packed the small pile into a silver pipe.

"I don't know . . ." I mumbled. I didn't do drugs, not since the sixties, when I had dabbled enough to know that I liked my life a lot better straight.

"Just one small puff." Her voice was satin.

She lit the pipe and inhaled deeply. The smoke circled me as she exhaled, as though coaxing me to try. And why not, I mused. Tourist-girl takes time out from it all.

I reached for the pipe. The silver bowl was heated, the scent rich as my butch cop's dark hair. I took a deep breath, sucking in the harsh sweet taste. It burned as it pushed into my lungs as if forcing each cell to expand into a dream.

"This is very good." Her words were thick honey. "I don't smoke often, but this is a special occasion, wouldn't you say?"

I nodded. My head felt light, yet heavy all at once. A sudden heat sifted through my body and I leaned into the plushness of the couch. I felt hazy, warm and very, very good.

"What do you think?" She brushed her lips on my cheek.

"I think," I said, wondering if my words sounded as cumbersome to her as they did to me, "that I like very much that you're a cop."

We both broke into giggles. I couldn't remember feeling this relaxed in a long time.

"Because I'm tough?" Her voice was suddenly cocky.

"No, because of the uniform. I like uniforms." Words were coming from grayness as I spoke.

"Do you want to see me in my uniform?" She looked me straight in the eye. Her mouth had curled into a devious smile.

"No, actually." I paused. The heaviness had seeped into my tongue. "I want *you* to see *me* in it." I smiled back with a look more devious than hers. Mine was a slick smile, a sly smile, a come-on-and-try-me smile.

Yeah. I liked the way I felt all right. I was hot. I was wicked. But I was crystal clear. I wouldn't cheat on my girl back home, I wouldn't fuck this woman, but I'd walk the edge. I'd walk the edge so damn close that it would almost count.

She grabbed my hand and led me to her bedroom. On the back of the door hung the dark blue uniform. I pulled the crisp shirt from the hanger.

"And your police belt?" I asked with an air of self-satisfaction. I had seen those belts that cops wore. The flashlight, the mace, the handcuffs, the gun — like large charms dangling from a thick leather bracelet.

Her belt hung haphazardly from an easy chair. I watched dreamily as she lifted the belt adorned with a billy club, a whistle, handcuffs. Only one holster remained empty.

"Is there a gun?" I reached for the belt. It was heavier than I had imagined.

She pulled a gun from her jacket, unloaded it,

checked it twice and pushed it into the vacant holster.

"Thirty-eight?" I whispered as I glanced to her full breasts. I ran my hand over the rough handle. *Thirty-eight.* Like sex on the beach, it was *that* kind of phrase. Loaded with intention, said for the sake of the words, and nothing else. I had no idea what a thirty-eight even looked like.

"Yeah, thirty-eight," she said thickly. Did I imagine her breasts swelling under her shirt? For a brief moment, I thought her sweater had lifted and her rounded breasts were unveiled, pendulous, tipped with large, dark-circled nipples.

"So," she said with feigned impatience. "Do I get to see you in this or not?"

I carried the uniform shirt and belt into the small bathroom. A subtle breeze of music drifted provocatively from the bedroom. Stripping out of my casual, blend-in, out-of-town-girl clothes, I slipped into the coarse uniform top and peered into the mirror at the stiff dark shirt decorated with letters, and raised the collar. I looked good.

The shirt barely covered my discreetly dampened black lace panties. I buttoned the shirt and strapped the belt which hung awkwardly, like you'd expect twenty pounds of leather and metal would hang, around my slender waist.

The curtains were drawn, and five candles lit the room. She was on the bed, had lit the pipe. The hypnotic scent swirled like a genie's magic.

"Have another taste." She leaned toward me, her dark eyes glittering as though bewitched.

As I drew in the hot smoke, the genie pulled me through a thick fog. "Come on," she chanted like a captivating siren. "Let go, out-of-town, close-to-the-edge-girl. Let go."

"Get your fucking feet off the bed," I snapped. I was thinking like a cop, feeling like a cop. There was power, there was control. I wore the gun, I made the rules.

She shifted her feet to the side of the bed and smiled in approval. "You look very hot," she murmured, her voice low. "I've never seen my uniform look so good."

I felt her words, like quick caresses. Sweet words weaken me like bouquets of flowers and gift-wrapped perfume. Was I pretty? I wondered, as I swayed to the music. Was I more than she had ever had?

The collar of her shirt grazed my neck, the belt hung low and heavy as I moved to the music. A slow beat, a steady beat, Depeche Mode sang desperate words about danger. And caught in the genie's steamy spell, I danced to please my butch audience.

"Take it off," coaxed the genie.

I closed my eyes and swayed like a canoe on a tranquil lake. Gently, erotically, I undulated. I carefully unbuttoned the first button, then the next.

"More. Let me see more." Her words, covert and enchanting, invaded the music and seemed to direct my fingers down the shirt. Each button escaped its captive hole, and the shirt, as if on its own, pulled open.

Her breathing was heavy as she stared intently at me. I opened the shirt and showed off my soft pink breasts. She shifted; the air was thick with desire.

"I like your billy club," I purred.

I pulled the billy club from the holster. I stroked its length. It was large, bulky against my hand. I was surprised at how smooth it was.

"You like cops?" I said with a dangerous edge. I tapped the billy club against my open palm.

She didn't answer. My butch girl had lit a cigarette and the tip glowed red, like my nipples, like my thickened clit.

"Yeah," I said in a spell. "I think perhaps you do."

I turned away, bent over, and lifted the black lace from my oily cunt. I spread my legs as I rubbed the head of the billy club against my throbbing wet clit. The tip was cool, smooth. It was nasty and I was hot. To the music, I swirled the bulb-shaped tip, to the music I rolled it. Bent over, leaning down, I could no longer see her cigarette tip. But I could hear her, oh yes, I could hear her. And she liked it.

"Jesus," she moaned.

I leaned over further, spread my legs wider. I wanted her to see everything I had. I wanted her to memorize the way the hard tip of her billy club looked smothered in my pussy.

I had visions of the countless arrests she would make as she pulled out her billy club, this billy club, my billy club. She'd stare at the thick stick, laced with traces of my dried white silk, and make demands of her prisoners.

"You'd like to be fucked by my billy club, wouldn't you, nasty girl?" she said as I pushed the tip further into my slit.

"Yes, oh yes," I moaned. I squatted, gliding the wood deeper inside.

"Playing police girl, all dressed up in blue." She

96

was behind me. She caught my nipple between her fingers and twisted it lightly.

The high from the weed had intensified. I was dizzy, lost in a maze of shadows and dim lights. The music blended with her words, thick words, which slurred into tiny heat waves between my pussy lips.

"Yeah, yeah," she muttered. "I like it too. Dressed up, breaking and entering . . ." She pulled the billy club from my hand.

"Say it," she demanded.

I heard her words as they meshed in the shadows. "Breaking and entering . . ." I whispered.

"And the billy club?" She dragged the billy club up my thigh, inch by slow inch. "You want the billy club?"

Her breath was hard as she poked the polished head of the club against my throbbing pussy. Spreading my tight walls, the thick, bulb-shaped tip pushed into my slit. I lunged into it, hungry to take in as much as I could.

She plucked my nipples, pinched them, then plunged the billy club deeper. Red hot darts stung through my body as she sunk in.

"Too deep," I gasped. "Easy."

She backed off. "You're the fucking cop," she smirked. "If you don't like it, arrest me."

I reached for the gun.

"You're under arrest," I said in a deep voice. "You're fucking under arrest." I stood in front of her, my cop shirt opened, the belt still dangling from my waist.

She put her hands up in the air.

Suddenly, a bright light flashed overhead. "What the hell?" a voice from behind me shouted.

In the doorway, a woman brandished a gun that was aimed directly at me.

"Thank God," the island woman stammered, her hands still up in the air. "She brought me here at gunpoint, forced me . . ." She broke into tears.

I stood, dumbfounded, still pointing the gun at the island woman.

"Drop the gun," the woman at the door said carefully.

I nodded then laid the gun on the bed. I was still too high, too confused by the brightness of the light, the suddenness of the events.

"I can explain," I muttered stupidly.

"You can explain why you broke into my home, put on my uniform and have this woman at gunpoint?" the woman said harshly.

I stared incredulously at the island woman. "We were playing a game. I thought this was her house —"

"And that's why you broke in?" the cop interrupted sarcastically. She tossed my bent credit card onto the floor. She said roughly to the island woman, "Go on, get the hell out of here."

The island woman shot me a quick look and hurried out the door.

"Got some ID?" The cop's voice was cold.

I reached into my back pocket, fumbled for my ID.

As the woman examined my license carefully, I took a moment to appraise her. She was taller than I, with short black hair combed back like a small-time hood. Her eyes tightened into a tough squint, emphasized by the severity of her thin-lipped mouth. An open pack of Kools rode the right pocket of her white shirt.

"Out-of-town girl, huh?" she asked, not looking up from my driver's license.

"I can explain," I said, wishing I were out of her uniform and back in my clothes.

"Can you, now?" Her eyes stared into mine, then blatantly drifted to my lace panties.

"Out-of-town girl, wrongly accused, victim of a local bully island cop, right?" she said, her words smoldering with desire. She took a step closer and touched her cool fingers to my face.

I felt weak in the knees. It's those rare occasions, when a self-confident woman comes on to me, that I'm an easy, easy girl.

"As a matter of fact," I said, admiring her strong build, her olive eyes. "It happens all the time."

Red Dragons

They were across the room. It was dark and the dance floor was packed, but I noticed them. Standing like they answered to no one, they leaned against the bar, they slammed their drinks.

I had come looking for bikers. Halloween dances brought them out, with their hard-edge attitudes and tough-woman eyes. Dressed in a fifties pink poodle skirt and a delicate pearl-buttoned cashmere sweater, I was every biker's dream.

At the bar, there were four women, a tight group, a closed clique. Costumed as biker chicks, their attention would shift from one another to the dancers then back again.

They were dressed as though they owned a neighborhood somewhere in New York City. Their sleeveless white T-shirts exposed strong arms that were painted with authentic-looking tattoos. Slicked-back hair, bandannas tied around their foreheads, silver chains with crosses around their necks — they emanated a don't-fuck-with-me attitude, a don't-fuck-with-me charisma.

Led by fantasies, I moved in the shadows, around the dancers. I was dressed in pink, vulnerable in pink, and my heart pounded as I crossed the room. The image of being held down, of being taken by bikers had led me to this dance. These women with their leather jackets tossed on the bar, their thick studded belts buckled around their waists, seemed to offer just that.

When I reached the bar, the last of the biker women pushed her glass across the smooth wood and followed the others out a side door. I appraised my reflection in the mirror. In my powder-puff pink outfit and my red hair pulled into a ponytail, I looked remarkably innocent. My pale complexion, graced with a spattering of freckles, added an overwhelmingly virtuous effect.

I wondered how those women, dressed as tough bikers, would treat a chaste girl from the fifties. Imagining being pushed, like that empty whiskey glass, from woman to woman, I headed out the side door after them.

Women dressed as clowns, as French maids, as hula girls, crowded the veranda. My biker women were nowhere to be seen.

"Excuse me, have you seen . . .?" The words swirled as I pushed through the women, too many women. On the porch, out in the night air, they were in my way.

Down the steps, onto the street, I hurried. With intentions, with fantasies unleashed, I scanned the street. In the distance, the subtle movement of shadows seduced my attention. Down the block, leaning against a beat-up car, they lounged.

I headed toward them. Saddle shoes and bobby socks, poodle skirt and pink lipstick, I crossed the street and entered their domain.

"What do you want, girlie?"

A stocky woman appraised me with piercing eyes. The bandanna around her arm partially hid a mock tattoo of a red dragon. Flames darted from the dragon's mouth, fire darted from the woman's eyes.

"Looks to me like the Halloween party has moved out here," I said. I gazed at her chain-laden, heavy black boots.

"Does it now?" She laughed. They all laughed.

There were the four women from the bar, plus two more. The six clever predators watched me carefully.

I was spinning. I could feel their eyes devour me. Pert beneath my cashmere sweater, my nipples were sharp from the cool night air, from their roving eyes.

"Can I join the party?" I said. My voice was a flurry of feathers.

"What kind of party are you looking for?" The stocky woman put her leather jacket on, raising the collar as she spoke.

"I think you know," I said, trembling. I felt suddenly cold.

I looked back at her boots, their boots. The group was well-costumed, all the way down to their metal studded footwear.

"Yeah, I think we know what she wants," the woman said, flashing me a quick wink.

The others laughed. The air snapped with heightened intensity. A surge of heat shot through me. My biker fantasy was coming true.

"So you want it?" a thick blonde woman said. Her drawn out words bordered burlesque.

I shook my head. "But I'm not consenting," I murmured coyly, thinking I can't wait.

"I thought not," the stocky woman teased, grabbing my sweater.

Round pearl buttons flew into the street. Not letting go, the woman stepped back, deliberately crushing two of the pearls beneath her black boot.

"I say we take the non-consenting lady for a ride," the woman said, her voice low.

I glanced at the car with mixed feelings. My friend, Gretchen, was back at the bar. She was used to me wandering from her side. But to actually leave without telling her?

"Let me tell my buddy I'm leaving and I'll be right back." I tried to move but the woman's grip tightened.

"What the fuck are you talking about?" She pushed me into the car.

I had to admit, this was my fantasy and it was evolving exactly the way I wanted. To go back to the bar now would blow the scene. Gretchen would understand.

The women pushed into the car, surrounded me, and we took off. Ignoring me, they laughed, told jokes. Within minutes we were at the end of a dirt road.

A woman dragged me out of the car. I was in heaven. How many women went to a costume ball and scored like this? A gang of bikers pushing me around at the end of some deserted road — how many women had the opportunity to act out this fantasy?

"Let's see her tits," someone said callously.

Yeah, I thought. Take a look at my tits.

A short, dark-haired woman ripped my sweater completely open while another held my arms behind my back.

"Oh, please don't," I said dramatically.

Pinned, I watched as the stocky woman flashed a knife in front of my face. With a quick motion she cut my pink lace bra down the center, exposing my small breasts.

My nipples hardened in delicious anguish. God, these women had put together great costumes. My panties were beginning to soak.

"Look at these tits." The woman pressed her cold fingers against my nipple and squeezed it unforgivingly.

"Nice," another said as she sucked my other nipple into her mouth.

One pinched as the other sucked hard. The sensation was unbearably arousing. I tried to arch forward, but the woman who held my arms was unremitting. I was unable to do anything but moan.

"Hey bobby-socks girl," someone shouted. "What you got up that pink poodle skirt?"

"Yeah," another called. "She got herself some cat up there?"

Some cat, I thought. My panties were thick with dampness. *Yes, pull up my skirt, take turns with me. I'm ready, ready, ready.*

"No, please," I whispered for effect.

The woman's grip was tight on my arms. The rough women at my breasts pulled back abruptly. My nipples stood fierce, burned like fire.

"I want her scent," the stocky woman said.

My captor pushed me over to a large flat boulder, laid me on the cool stone. The women held me down, lifted my poodle skirt, spread my legs.

I was delirious. They could have me, they could fuck me, they could do whatever the hell they wanted.

"Okay, Jay," someone said.

The stocky woman stepped between my spread legs and two women lifted them high while two others hoisted my hips. Jay put her hands on the inside of my thighs to pull me apart even further and then put her face close to my drenched panties.

"Fucking wet bitch!" Jay laughed. I could feel her heated breath caress my thighs as she spoke. Her nose, her mouth, her lips grazed my panties lightly. My clit was swollen, anxious to be exhibited.

"She wants it, Jay."

"It's con-sen-su-al, Jay."

"Give it to her, Jay."

"You want it, girlie?" Jay looked me straight in the eyes.

My legs ached slightly from being held apart. My back pressed uncomfortably into the stone. Did I want it? Yes!

My look scorched hers and I shook my head. After all, drama was drama.

Jay backed off. "I don't want her till she fucking begs for it."

The other women surrounded me.

"You got a problem?"

"You gotta fucking problem, bitch?"

My legs were still held apart and a woman ran her fingers up and down the lace crotch of my panties. Another kissed me more tenderly than I would have thought, another roughly pulled at my nipples, sucked at my nipples.

My clit throbbed against the stretched panty material. I ached to be touched, ached to have fingers separate me, open me, beat against my raised flesh, poke into my juiced-up slit.

"Okay yes, okay yes," I moaned.

"Fuck that shit," Jay called from somewhere.

"She said beg." The woman whose fingers teased my panties grabbed the sopping material and sliced it with a knife.

The cool air licked my pussy. My wetness held me together like sugar glue.

"Open me, please open me!" I cried. I desperately wanted my thick lips pulled, cleaved. I wanted them to see my desire. I was engorged. I was blood-flushed. I was knotted and ready.

Someone pulled my lips open, another ran the butt of the knife between my slippery lips. I was crazy with desire.

"Fuck her."

"Yeah, fuck her!"

"Yes please, please, please." I tried to push my cunt against the rounded knife handle. The women appeased me, held me open, and one of them inserted the bulky, rough handled knife slightly into my cream filled slit.

"Easy does it, firecracker," the woman snickered. She rotated the handle, barely in my entrance, with small circular movements.

"Fuck me, please," I begged.

"Sounds to me like she's begging for it, Jay."

"Yes, begging, yes, I'm begging."

Jay pushed her way between my legs. The other women gave her space.

Her pants were unzipped and a dildo stood out from her opened jeans. She jammed her fingers into my dampness and smeared my grease across the dildo's bulbous head.

My pussy pounded. I felt thick and extended. Every nerve ending pulsated wildly.

Jay grabbed my hips. Her fingers dug brutally into my skin.

"I hate to see a woman beg," she said, ramming the dildo deep into my tightly stretched pussy.

They held me, they watched, their breathing coarsened into quick panting. I was beyond myself in the stinging pleasure.

Plunging into me, relentless, she simultaneously held my hips. I cried in pleasure, I moaned in pain. It was good, it was bad, it was nice, it was brutal.

"Oh yes, oh yes," I screamed.

The dildo tunneled into me. Drilling deep, she opened me, stretched me, dove into me in fast penetrating movements. And all the while, her electric-green eyes pierced into mine.

The women held me down. My only permissible response was to bounce, under Jay's direction, on her reaming spear. Starting to enter a hard come, I desperately tried to break free, to no avail. I was a prisoner, impaled on her gouging, thick harpoon.

The pleasure spilled out as I screamed Jay's name, over and over, into the night.

On the way back to the bar, they laughed, told stories, but no one said a word to me. I figured that once we got to the club, we'd all have a drink now that the party was over. But instead, when we arrived, they pushed me out of the car and sped into the night.

"Where the hell have you been?" Gretchen caught up to me as soon as I walked in the door.

"Halloween party," I said, not hiding my exhilaration.

She appraised my torn sweater, haphazardly closed by the two remaining buttons. "Oh yeah? With whom?"

"Did you see the women who were dressed in biker costumes?" My voice was laden with excitement. "We had quite a party."

"You left with those women! Are you crazy? They're the Red Dragons!" Gretchen turned white.

"The who?" I asked, remembering the dragon tattoo on Jay's arm. The tattoo I thought had been painted.

"Only the roughest women in L.A.," Gretchen said. "They're into, you know, all that kinky . . ."

Gretchen kept talking, but I had stopped listening. I was lost in ecstasy, anticipating that moment when a Red Dragon would be tattooed onto my arm.

Eternity Girl Seeks . . .

On Valentine's eve, the doorbell rang. Regina clicked the VCR pause button. She wasn't expecting anyone, especially since her recent breakup with Harriet. She had planned on another long evening lost in her taped episodes of *All My Children* and *General Hospital*.

"Yeah?" she called loudly as she peered into the peephole.

A dark-haired woman, holding a bouquet of

flowers, stood on the porch. "Delivery from Cradle's Florist."

Regina opened the door.

"You Regina Myers?" the delivery woman asked.

"Yeah, thanks." Regina reached for the flowers. Three long-stemmed red roses, surrounded by teeny lace-like flowers, were gathered by a purple ribbon. Stapled to the ribbon was a purple envelope.

"Happy Valentine's Day," the delivery woman said with a light smile.

Regina gave her a quick nod and closed the door.

"Oh, Harriet," Regina said wistfully as she opened the envelope.

Even though Harriet had broken her heart, there was still a part of Regina that hoped Harriet would realize what she had lost and come back. Perhaps the affair with the other woman had fizzled? Perhaps Harriet missed her desperately? Even after the pain, even after the humiliation, Regina knew she would take her back if Harriet asked.

A provocative unfamiliar scent swirled from the white stationery that had been neatly folded into the envelope. Sitting on the couch, Regina read the note.

For Regina,
This token of the earth is for you.
Given not from a lover of your past
nor your present, but from someone
who is intrigued by your apparent
love of life and the pleasures it
can bestow.

The revelation of my identity is
inappropriate to share with you

at this present time, but perhaps
sometime in the future . . .

Happy Valentine's Day.

Absentmindedly, Regina clicked the television off.
The flowers were not from Harriet, Regina was
certain. This was not her scent, this was not her
style, and these were definitely not her words.

Regina tried to identify the fragrance without
success. With rich exotic spices, tantalizing floral
blends, the perfume was deliciously unknown.

"I have a secret admirer!" Regina said with a
laugh.

She reread the note.

This gift from the earth is for you. Someone with
earth-consciousness, Regina reasoned.

Not from lover past or present. There was no
present lover and the past lovers . . . well, they
weren't going to send Regina flowers, that was for
sure. It was someone new.

Intrigued by love of life. Someone who senses my
spirit, my zest, Regina supposed.

After all, Harriet had never understood her true
essence, her love of life. It was a pleasant change to
hear from someone who did.

But who?

The woman was intelligent — that was obvious
from her well-thought out, well-written note. She
was someone who went after what she wanted in a
fascinating way. She had style, she had mystery, she
had patience. Above all, she had Regina thoroughly
intrigued.

A job well done, Regina thought, impressed by

the note and its captivating vagueness. With a smile she reached for the phone book.

Mystery had its allure, but as far as Regina was concerned, its appeal was short-lived. Within minutes she had Cradle's Florist on the line.

"You delivered flowers to me this evening," Regina said sweetly. "And I can't read the signature. Is there any way you can tell me who sent them?"

"Give me a minute," the florist said after getting Regina's name and address.

Regina closed her eyes and inhaled the intoxicating scent from the stationery. Soon enough she'd have this puzzle solved.

"I'm so sorry," the florist said sympathetically. "The woman who bought the flowers paid cash. No way to know her name."

"Wait, is that the one with the purple envelope?" Regina heard a woman in the background say. "Didn't she say her boss had sent her?"

"Oh yes, her boss," the florist said to Regina. "Looks like the woman was doing an errand for her boss. That's all I can tell you."

"Could you tell me what she looked like?" Regina asked, disappointed.

"Do you remember the woman?" the florist asked her partner.

"Brownish, I think," the woman answered. "There've been so many orders today, it's hard to remember."

"She thinks the woman was a brunette," the florist said. "That's about it."

"Well, thanks anyway." Regina was frustrated.

She scanned the note. There were no clues, no hints, nothing except the bewitching perfume. Hoping to preserve its scent, Regina placed the note in a baggie. She had every intention of solving this mystery.

"I can't figure out who'd write me a note like that." Regina glanced out of Ellie's window to the street below. The constant downpour normally would have depressed her, but not today, not after last night's delicious mystery.

"Brunette, huh . . ." Ellie sipped her tea. She had said she was glad to see Regina in better spirits, especially since the breakup with Harriet had been so sudden and painful.

Ellie and Regina had become quite close the last year and had spent many hours gossiping over tea. Even so, Ellie still had trouble understanding the dynamics of the complicated lesbian relationships Regina involved herself in. Not that Ellie's relationship with Harold had been a bed of roses, Regina mused.

"Maybe Harriet's sorry," Ellie offered. "Maybe she's seen the light, realized what she's lost. After all, you're quite a catch. A few weeks away from you and she's probably devastated." Ellie sipped her tea carefully. "Maybe Harriet had someone purchase the flowers for her —"

"Not Harriet's style," Regina interrupted. Her eyes focused on Ellie momentarily and then moved to the delicate teacup balanced like a bird's nest between Ellie's slender fingers.

When Ellie and her husband had moved into the four-plex, Regina was immediately regretful that

Ellie was married to a man — but she and Ellie had found that they shared more in common than not. Their friendship had blossomed and on many occasions, Regina and Harriet had joined Ellie and her husband for dinner or a movie.

Regina had had a dazzling infatuation with Ellie from the start. But Ellie, in her good-natured way, had made it clear that she was not attracted to women . . . ("Such a thing is implausible, really," she had said, not looking Regina in the eyes.) Besides, she and Harold were unalterably faithful to each other.

To this day, Regina was still occasionally thrown off balance by Ellie's arresting beauty. As if she were an exquisite doll, her dark, loose curls were tied back with a thin ribbon, her eyes were brilliant sapphires, her high cheeks were dusted with rosy hues.

"What about that delivery woman from Jake's Pizza?" Ellie placed the teacup on the table. "Don't you have a crush on her?"

"Yeah," Regina said with a laugh. "A crush on her and twenty other women, none of whom give me the time of day."

"Well, I certainly can't imagine that," Ellie said with a smile. "Someone out there definitely has a crush on you."

Marley, Ellie's thick-furred cat, jumped onto Ellie's lap and burrowed a place between her full breasts. Regina watched for a moment, envious, then glanced out at the rain-soaked street.

A crush on me, Regina thought, fascinated. Imagine that.

* * * * *

Back in her apartment, Regina reread the note. Although somewhat faded, the fragrance still lingered.

Given not from a lover past or present but from someone who is intrigued by your apparent love of life. There's got to be some clue, some tip-off, Regina thought, examining the words.

She could take the note to the Perfumery to identify the scent. She could . . .

And there, in that moment, she saw it. Each time the letter *f* was typed, the bottom of the letter was missing its little platform, its serif. Her secret admirer's typewriter had a noticeably flawed letter *f*.

Regina put the note back into the baggie, grabbed her jacket and hurried out the door.

"So I went to the Perfumery and the scent is —" Regina bowed ceremoniously for effect — "Eternity for Women!"

"Well, if that isn't a coincidence . . ." Ellie started to say but was interrupted by Regina's enthusiasm.

"So I've got this great idea!" She tossed her jacket on Ellie's couch. "I'm going to put an ad in *Women's News* and post a notice on the community board. You know, like in that movie, *Desperately Seeking Susan*? Yeah, I got the ad all figured out: 'Eternity girl seeks the bottom of the letter *f*.'" Regina was out of breath. "You have a typewriter I can borrow?"

Confusion swept Ellie's face. "I'm not quite sure where Harold's stashed it."

She hesitated a moment, then headed toward the bedroom. After a few minutes, she returned, her arms locked around the typewriter and her face ashen. She looked as though she had suddenly taken ill.

"You okay, Ellie?"

"Yeah, I . . ." Her voice fell away. There were tears in her eyes.

Regina rushed to her, pried the typewriter from her arms, and held her tight. "What is it, Ellie? What's happened?"

Regina had never held Ellie in her arms, had never run her fingers in her cocoa-shaded hair, had never felt the fullness of Ellie's breasts against her own.

She felt as if she were swirling in a summer breeze — what with the softness, the intoxicating scent of Ellie's hair. It was a rich, exotic scent, somehow haunting. Regina soared, spellbound. She was lost in the dark storm of perfumed hair.

"I need to be alone. I need to think." Ellie pulled away, stumbling over her words.

"Ellie, you can talk to me. You know that, don't you?" Regina stepped back. She had a stabbing fear that Ellie, conscious of the momentary haze of desire, would push her away.

"I'm okay, really," Ellie said with a vague smile. Unnaturally remote, she motioned to the typewriter. "Come back when you've finished your ad."

* * * * *

118

Eternity girl seeks bottom to the letter . . . As Regina typed the words for her ad, her thoughts drifted to Ellie. What could have upset her so? What would have provoked her sudden tears?

Regina floated back to those few precious moments when she had become suffused in Ellie's perfumed softness. Now that Regina had a moment to think clearly, Ellie's light perfume was oddly similar to the scent that had been sprayed on the note.

Regina felt a free-falling sensation in her stomach. Was Ellie's subtle scent *the* scent? Was Ellie the one? Had she cried because she couldn't find the words, had no idea how to approach Regina, could not come to terms with her newfound feelings?

Regina examined the words she had typed: *Eternity girl seeks bottom to the letter* . . . Regina hit the key. The letter printed clearly, except the missing serif.

A low whistle passed Regina's lips. "Well, I'll be damned!"

"Ellie?" Regina pounded on Ellie's door. "Ellie, it's me."

The door opened and Ellie appeared like a sensuous angel, with dazzling hair and pearl-colored skin. Her pale pink lips trembled slightly.

"You know?" Ellie whispered.

"Oh, sweet one." Regina took Ellie into her arms. "I didn't realize . . . this must be so difficult for you."

Ellie nodded. "I just need to be held."

Regina was captivated by Ellie's smooth skin, the warmth of her body. Consumed by Ellie's lusciousness, Regina felt her legs momentarily weaken, as though she might teeter to the floor, as though she might melt into oblivion.

"This was so unexpected . . . Harold and I had made promises, had a certain trust . . ." Ellie spoke in small sporadic bursts.

"Sometimes things, unforeseeable things, happen that no one can understand." Regina pushed her fingers into the darkness of Ellie's hair, as though to capture the richness from each strand.

She pressed her mouth against Ellie's throat, buried her lips against the satin skin, the silken hair, the shapely shoulders.

"Oh Ellie, Ellie, Ellie," Regina whispered between kisses, fire-laced kisses. Along Ellie's ivory neck, across her tear-stained cheeks and finally to her plush, petaled mouth, Regina smothered Ellie with kisses.

Ellie, like willow branches flirting with spring, moved with Regina. She swayed with each kiss, opened with each kiss, gave way to the heated breath of each kiss.

Seduced, bewitched by potent woman-love, Ellie slipped her tongue between Regina's warm lips and explored the warm folds of Regina's mouth. She thought only of Regina's kiss, Regina's sweet touch, Regina's soft breasts pressed against her own. Her nipples burned, her breathing heightened.

Engulfed in a hot haze, they tumbled to the floor. Regina lifted Ellie's sweater, unhooked her white lace bra, ran her hands against Ellie's pale pink breasts. The nipples immediately tightened into burnt-red pellets.

"How long I've wanted you, how long I've waited." The words, without thought, tumbled from Regina's lips.

Regina gently squeezed the puckered nipples with her lips and Ellie let out a small whimper. Slowly, Regina caressed each nipple with her tongue. The areola was rigid, the red nipple distended and hard.

"I want to make love with you," Regina whispered as she inched a trail of kisses between Ellie's breasts.

Pulling Ellie's drawstring pants out of her way, Regina moved her hand along the soft roundness. Teasing her fingers across the slight belly button, she then continued into the silky hair.

As her fingers explored further, they reached where the flesh cleaved. The covering fringe was warm with the thick, slippery juices that had seeped from within the folds.

Regina dampened her fingertips in, swirling the syrupy fluid between her fingers, then burrowed into the wet interior of the hair-matted folds.

Ellie spread her legs and her vulva opened wide. The smoky scent of her skin, the sultry fragrance from her viscous pussy sap created an entrancing cologne.

Regina's fingers kissed the pulp between the folds and her clitoral skin became noticeably hardened. She then captured a large lip between her fingers and pulled it firmly. She slid her fingers up and down the lip, tugging different sections with each movement.

As if desperate for more, Ellie raised her hips.

Regina peeled the lip back and took in the beauty of Ellie's pink fruit cup.

The clitoral hood was thin and blush-rose, yet the tiny clit, which was a flushed dark red, strained recklessly from the flaccid pink backdrop.

Regina knelt to caress the tiny knot of flesh with her tongue. The addictive taste was heated sweet-spice. She stretched the lips further and buried her tongue into Ellie's raven-haired mystery.

Flicking her tongue, Regina massaged the right side of the tiny shaft, fluttered lightly over the tiny head then slathered the thick vaginal opening.

Ellie spread her knees further and her legs fell to each side. The sexual intensity was staggering. Her pussy was the color of fire. As Regina's tongue sliced into her then darted across her pulsating clitoris, Ellie moaned, ignited into mounting, incessant, furious flames of passion. She dug her fingers into the carpet. She grabbed wildly at Regina's short brown hair.

Regina, lost in the darkness, her face sex-drenched, continued to tease Ellie's widened opening. She did not deviate from her persistent rhythm. She drove into the fullness of Ellie's sex then pulled out to tease the dark clit with fast cat-tongue licks.

Ellie was sugar. Ellie was sweet cream. A voluptuous goddess, a soft kitten, a jeweled nymph, a compelling siren — Ellie's pussy surrounded, engulfed, swallowed Regina.

"All of you all of you all of you all of you," Regina muttered.

Ellie was suddenly still, as if she could not move,

would not move. She quivered, she trembled, she shook.

The throbbing convoluted into pulsating, twisted spasms, coiled into pounding contractions. Regina could feel as Ellie was dragged to the heights, spun in the air and tossed to the ground. And finally, in an unimaginable crescendo, she surrendered to Regina's unyielding mouth.

"When did you decide you wanted me?" Regina ran her fingers across Ellie's still sex-flushed breasts.

"I suppose unconsciously I always have," Ellie said quietly. "It's just that when you asked for the typewriter and I —"

"And you knew I'd figure out that you had written the note . . ." Regina interrupted.

At that moment, the apartment door opened and a shocked Harold stood frozen in the doorway. Harriet, with a sick look on her face, was at his side.

"What the hell!" He tossed the package he was carrying across the room. There was the sound of glass breaking as the package hit the wall and a concentrated breeze of Eternity filled the room.

"Oh, don't you dare!" Ellie shouted as she pulled her sweater on and climbed into her pants. "Don't you *even* dare! What's the matter? Is Harold upset that I got to his secret fantasy girl first?"

"What?" Regina said, confused.

"What the hell . . .?" Harold muttered.

"Yeah, what the hell. I found your follow-up to

the first love letter in the typewriter. 'My identity is soon to be revealed.' Don't think I don't know what you've been up to!"

Harriet's face paled. "Oh, Christ," she moaned. She looked at Regina who sat, flabbergasted, on the floor. "I borrowed the typewriter from Harold, I wrote the note. I realized that I had . . ."

"We're through, Ellie!" Harold screamed as he turned toward the door.

"I only wanted another chance," Harriet said, ignoring Harold's departure. "I thought if I made it seem like it was someone new . . . and I am new, I've changed, Regina. We could start fresh, we could work things . . ."

Astounded, Regina turned to Ellie. "I thought you wrote the note."

"I thought Harold . . ." Ellie said, stunned. "I thought he had betrayed me. I thought you had figured that out too and had come up to comfort me."

"Well, Regina?" Harriet gave Ellie a distasteful glare. "Are you coming?"

Regina touched Ellie's face. "Are you going to be all right?"

Ellie stared at the tiny green specks in the carpet. She pulled at the short strands of carpet as though searching for something.

"Perhaps you should go after Harold . . . explain things —" Harriet urged. She shot a 'let's-wrap-this-up' look to Regina. "These things can always be worked out. You'll be okay —"

"Oh, but things *have* worked out," Ellie

interrupted. Her eyes seemed to flash with a new intensity. "This is what I've desired for what seems like an eternity." She rested her hand lightly on Regina's. "And yes, I'm going to be *very* okay."

She Doesn't Care

The sound wakes me from my dream. The house is quiet and the clock glows: one a.m. I listen to the darkness. Have I just been dreaming? Was there someone at the door? I am enveloped by the eerie green glow from the clock. Certainly, it was a dream and there is no one there.

The house is quiet and I lie in bed listening to the blackness. I contemplate wandering down the hall to the front door but the doorbell does not ring again.

I lie in bed yet I seem to watch myself move

down the hall to the living room. I peer out the front window. There is nothing but the dim glow of the street light. Motionless, I am unable to turn away. I hear a slight tapping and tiptoe to the door.

"Let me in," she says, then the house falls silent. "Let me in, let me in."

She is in the house. I did not open the door yet she is next to me. Her perfume surrounds me and I feel drugged. She has entered my house though I have not opened the door. Somehow she has come in.

"I've missed you," she says. I am shadowed into her. She pushes into me and presses me against the wall. The wall is cold and her body is warm. Her body is hard and I'm flush against the wall. Her mouth, her hot mouth, is over mine. Her breath is my breath, her tongue is my tongue, her moan is my moan.

"You are mine." Her mouth whispers into mine.

I can't speak. Her mouth covers mine and I can't say no. If she stepped back, if she stepped back and waited, it wouldn't matter. I would have no words, I would not say no. I don't care.

Her hands rip at my T-shirt. They are rough against my breasts and her teeth bite into my neck. I don't care.

"You are mine!" she insists.

It is one o'clock and I am naked except for a thin shirt. Pressed against the cold wall, hostage to her passion. I don't care.

This is what I want. This is what I've wanted for months. She has come. She has broken the rules. I am no longer hers. I have a new lover who says she loves me, who trusts that I'm home alone. I don't care.

There is only the heat. There are only her hands. She lifts me. She carries me to the couch and she wraps my legs around her shoulders. She dives, she sinks, she drowns between my legs.

She moans but her sound is muffled. I am wet, I am crazy from the creaming of her hard tongue. She knows me, has always known me. I want her to keep the motion. She slices her tongue up and down in my gel. I am sugared, I am spiced, I am not hers and I don't care.

It is her tongue that makes the choices now. It is her tongue that makes the demands. She slashes it across my engorged flesh and I suffer the pleasure.

She knows the way. She remembers to keep far to the left, high on the tiny shaft. She stays high to the left with her tongue's pointed tip and I crash into agony. Deliriously, in sweet pain from her delicious torture, I know how close she is to home.

She teases me, has teased me forever. I grab her head and jam it into my sex-soaked flesh. I want her tongue-point on the tip of my clit. I want it now.

"Where's your girlfriend?" she mutters.

"I don't care."

"Don't care, huh?" she smirks. "Don't care cause she can't do it for you like I do, huh?" I can see the white of her teeth, the sparkle in her eyes.

She buries her tongue in my folds and presses hard. I want her to lick. I want her to lap across my brick-hard clit.

"Not like you. Never like you."

"No, never," she repeats. Her words are slippery. Her words are pussy-drenched.

Her tongue is a point. Her tongue is hard. She ribs it. She flicks it. She whips across my sex. I cry for it, pant for it, scream for it.

"Please, please, please, please."

Her tongue becomes lightning, a wind storm, a whirlpool. Ongoing, she does me. Unending, she works me.

My legs are stretched wide. I am open like never before.

"And that! And that! And that! And that!" I scream. I shudder. I tighten. I am hers.

I lie in my bed. The room is thick with sex. My fingers are wet and sweat dampens my thighs. She was here, I could feel her — hasn't left, I know it. I float from bed, soar down the hall. I think briefly of my girlfriend but I don't care.

She has made me come, but I'm still hot. She knows this about me. She takes care of me, always.

"Stacy doesn't know you like *I* do," she smirks. "Bet she doesn't carry one of these in her back pocket, either." She bends me over the side of a chair and spreads my legs apart.

She is rough with me, she is hard with me. She knows how to take me and I don't care what she does. She uses this as part of the edge, part of the high.

She digs her nails into the soft flesh.

"Like this?" she asks. "You like it like this?"

I am pulled apart and she squirts cool lube. She rubs the blunt end of the sheathed butt plug against my tightened sphincter. I try to relax because I want it easy, yet all the same, I rebel.

"Fuck you good, fuck you so good, don't I?" she says. She demands.

"Yeah, baby, yeah." I lift my ass, spread my legs further. I want it fast, but I want it easy.

"Like this," she insists and teases the plug into my resistant crevice.

I jerk. She hurts me with the pressure. I feel torn apart. I hate it, I ache, yet I am more pleased than ever.

"Does Stacy fuck you like this?" She jams the thick plug in and out of me.

"No, never," I cry.

"Not like my little girl likes it, huh?"

"Never," I mutter as I grab the sides of the chair, as I lift my ass even higher.

She stops, holds the plug still, deep inside me.

"Oh, God, yes," I moan, because I know, I know all too well what she will do next.

"Don't move, baby," she whispers. "Don't do a thing till I say."

The room is quiet. I do not move.

"Now tighten way down, baby."

I can feel her twist the plug incredibly slowly.

"That's right sugar, tightened way down . . ."

She turns the plug, tugs the plug in small rapid jerks. I am filled with an unbearable pleasure throughout my body. I bear down with all that I have, clenching the hard plug between the tender walls of my ass.

"And what about this?" she teases. The plug begins to vibrate. This was new. She had never inserted a vibrator before.

The sensations burn through me and I ram against the thick vibrating tool.

"Yeah, like that, like that!" I cry as I rotate, as I bob, as I have my way with the trespasser.

I grab the chair, my head buries into the cushion, my ass tilts to the ceiling. As she plunges, I squeeze. As she rams, I jerk, until I come like never before.

"You betrayed her," she whispers. I turn to face her but she is gone. I am grasping the chair, covered with sweat, alone in the dark room.

Had I really opened the door or was I dreaming? I wander down the hall and watch as I float into bed.

"You'd betray her?" I whisper.

The house is quiet, the clock glows one-thirty a.m. I reach for the phone. I could call her. No one would have to know. It's what I want and I don't care.

Illusions

After Rebecca left me — "I swear to you, this time it's over for good," she had threatened — I was more than ready to let her go. Rebecca and I had been lovers for the past two years. She was my first woman, my first love, and I tenaciously held onto our volatile thunder-and-lightning relationship until I couldn't take any more.

Rebecca had an angry streak that ran like an underwater stream and no matter what I did, it surfaced. I tried everything to make Rebecca happy, but it was never enough. Finally, after an explosive storm of brutal anger, Rebecca left me "once and for all." Good riddance, Rebecca.

I admit, at first I was apprehensive, having no idea how to be single in a lesbian world. Rebecca was the only woman I had ever been with and the thought of cruising into the lesbian nights was unnerving.

Yet in bed, I would waltz through richly embroidered fantasies of women, lots of women. On my arm, in my bed, women moaned my name in pleasure. At night, in the safety of my illusions, I became a tigress on the prowl.

After six weeks of whispering hot words to the darkness, my arms clasping my perfume-scented pillow, I decided the time had arrived. I was ready to cash in my fantasy world for the real thing. I wanted a woman.

I wanted a woman, and then another, and another. The possibilities seemed endless. I was single. I was attractive. I was hot. And I was ready.

The bars. That's where the women that spun the fantasies went. Cognac and warm whiskey heated them as their eyes scanned the darkness in search of flash. I knew this. Rebecca had woven her stories of the bars, these women, for me to admire.

Countless nights, lying in the cool darkness, Rebecca whispered of the women she had met before me, the women she had had. She spoke of their stickiness and their sighs, their desires and their climaxes, and her tongue would lash at my neck, her finger smooth across my hardened clitoris.

Although Rebecca was gone, the visions of the women, the sweet images she wove for me, still lingered, still called to me in my nighttime mirage.

Single, hungry and on fire with dreams, I went to the bars. But the reality and the fantasy quickly collided. There were women, lots of women, but not one of them interested in me.

Friday and Saturday nights, I wandered through the flashing shadows. I sat on stools, leaned against corners, gazed into crowded dance floors, disillusioned.

Where were the women with the diamond eyes? The women with the come-get-me attitude? The women who would look at me like Rebecca had said they looked at her? Not in these bars, not where I spent my empty nights.

One night, on a fluke, I entered a small bar off Castro. There was no dancing, no loud music, just a string of dim lights that lined the crease where the walls folded into the ceiling.

I was sitting in a corner, watching a blonde cruise a brunette as she played pool, when a woman passed in front of me. She didn't turn toward me, but when she reached the bar, when she stood under the lights, I saw her face.

There were no diamonds in her eyes. There was no come-get-me attitude. But her look was charged with challenge. Her features, compellingly hard, yet interestingly slick, caught my attention. Her eyes had a James Dean squint and her spiked hair was dark, cut with an angle that accentuated her tough-boy look. She wore a white T-shirt that stretched tight against her well-muscled body and firm pointed breasts. Tight black pegged jeans clipped her ass with intention.

I imagined she was part Indian; her cheek bones were high, her face square. Perhaps she was part

Greek with her olive complexion, with a hint of Latin full lips and fiery eyes. She leaned against the bar like a stud, a young Brando. She owned the place, or so her attitude insisted. She mattered, she made the choices, and that was that.

I tried to win her attention. I imagined diamonds in my eyes, a come-get-me attitude. I looked at her, like women, countless women, must have looked at Rebecca over the years.

The woman, with the tight T-shirt that made delicious promises, cast a quick glance toward me, my corner. I tilted my face like Garbo, I shifted my body like a haute-couture model. But the woman's eyes — had we even made eye contact? — then darted to the pool table.

What did a woman have to do? Rebecca had said eye contact sent women messages. My eyes must have betrayed me.

I glanced toward the pool table. The brunette was flirting with the blonde. I peeked back at the woman. Her black jeans formed a dark arrow that ended at her black boots, boots with silver tips, silver spurs.

I inhaled deeply and thought of Rebecca and her stories. How would this story have unraveled if she were whispering it to me in the night? "The woman would not make eye contact with me," Rebecca would have said. "No matter what I did. I wanted her, you know how I get, so I . . . so I . . ."

So she what? I deliberated. She what? She what? She what?

I imagined Rebecca's cognacs as I placed my drink on the table. "My eyes sparkle like diamonds,"

I chanted silently, attempting to muster Rebecca's come-hither look.

Taking a last deep breath, I took a step toward the woman, the shadow of Rebecca coaching me all the way.

"Are you waiting for someone?" I motioned to the empty stool next to the woman.

I watched her gaze slide from my face toward my boots and then back. "Not really," she said, detached.

I looked the woman in the eye and fantasized. *"Are you ready for some company?"* I might say.

"How ready?" she'd reply in the fantasy, grabbing my waist. *"As in do I want you? As in do I want to take you to my car and have you there? Or in the grass? Or right here on the bar?"*

"Hmmm." I stared at the stool.

"It's all yours." She pulled the seat out from the bar.

I sat next to her and glanced at the women playing pool, as if their game was of interest to me. From the corner of my eye, I watched only her.

This is it, I thought. I'm sitting next to my first conquest. I looked quickly at her silver spurs. If only I could find the right words. Rebecca had said women are always available, that success is simply a matter of approach. Like dancing, there's a lead and a follower. If you're a good lead, the follower just falls into the movement.

Like dancing. I stole another glance at the woman who was staring ahead. She, evidently, was not going to lead.

"Do you dance?" I said nonchalantly, although my heart was pounding so loudly that I could barely

137

hear myself. "I was thinking of going over to the Detour."

The light flirted in the woman's eyes as she turned toward me. "Do I dance?" she repeated, her expression almost smug. Her full lips curled provocatively. She swallowed her drink in one quick gulp and pushed the shot glass onto the bar. "Only if I can lead."

Hallelujah, Rebecca!

Her name was Marlo and she was stunning. When we left the bar, women stared after her as we passed. It was her look, heated and sharp; it was her walk, strong and determined; it was her eyes, noncommittal and challenging, that caused women to turn their heads, to slip into passing fantasies.

I followed her across the bar, my eyes shifting from the women's wistful looks to Marlo's impressive arms. She had swung her leather jacket over her shoulder and her biceps bulged noticeably.

"Drive over together?" she proposed, although the intriguing squint of her coffee-colored eyes suggested a toss in a queen-sized bed laden with feather pillows.

Rebecca once told me a story about a woman she had met in a bar. "I don't ordinarily leave bars with women I don't know," she had admitted. "But this was one of those times when it seemed okay to cross that line. We got into this woman's car, her name was Desiree or something like that, and within seconds, she was all over me."

Within seconds, I thought, filling with desire. My

eyes skimmed to Marlo's thick arms, then to her thin T-shirt that flaunted her sable-colored nipples.

Do you want it? Right here in my car? I could fuck you hard. Look at my arms. Do you like a woman who looks like she means business? I mean business.

Marlo glanced at her watch. "On second thought, let's meet there. I need to make a stop."

Her words needled my fantasy. My imagined scenario, spread-eagled in the back of her car, her powerful biceps thrusting thick fingers into me, immediately deflated into a dark puddle.

"Sure," I said nonchalantly, hoping to camouflage my disappointment.

"If for some reason we miss each other —" She pulled a card from her back pocket — "give me a call sometime."

Was my face as pale as my mood had suddenly become? My allure had obviously faded. Marlo was moving on, to something bigger, something better. And I, decidedly, was going home.

Marlo opens the car door for me, and I slide into the seat. I am tingling with silver heat. She wants me, it's written all over her face. I doubt if we'll even get out of this parking lot.

Marlo, in the driver's seat, reaches for me. Her hands push into my hair.

"You are so beautiful." Her voice has a marked urgency to it.

She traces her fingers across my lips and lightly presses my mouth. She is timid as she gently forces her fingertip between my lips.

"So sweet," she whispers, prying into the dampness, running her finger against my tongue.

I ache with desire for her, tortured by the insistent craving between my legs. She pushes me back against the seat; her strong hands rush under my skirt.

"Marlo, yes, please," I plead.

I want her to pull my nipples. I want her to suck them until they are raw with pleasure. She pinches the sensitive skin. She tugs the nipple between her teeth.

I reach for her blindly, eager to lift her tightly stretched T-shirt. The shirt that has teased me, and every other woman in the bar, all night. I want to see the ebony nipples. I want to savor their beauty.

I pull at her shirt, but she grabs my hand, not letting me touch her, not letting me feast on her dark-tipped breasts.

"Oh yeah?" I say, tough.

"Yeah," she says, her strong arms pushing my hands away.

"Yes, oh yes," I called into the darkness of my room. I grabbed my pillow with one arm as the vibrator shuddered on my hardened pussy. "Marlo, please let me see them, please let me touch them."

I clamped my legs together and rocked into pleasure.

Marlo was my first thought the next morning. I reached to the nightstand where I had left her card and ran my finger across the raised burgundy letters of her name.

Perhaps I had been impulsive, coming straight

home, not bothering to stop at the Detour. Jumping to conclusions, I assumed Marlo had lost interest.

I considered my options. My thoughts drifted to Rebecca, who by now had probably already had countless adventures, then to the pillow I had clamped onto in last night's fantasy.

"This has gone too far," I said to the pillow and tossed it across the room. "You and I are through."

I dialed Marlo's number.

On the phone I had been sharp, cool, alluring. It was familiar to sit in the safety of my bedroom and play a role, coast on the possibilities, daring Marlo with clever comebacks and a nonchalant demeanor as if I were an expert with women like her, as if I were an expert with any woman.

Now, waiting for Marlo in a restaurant, I was besieged by a flurry of insecurities. What if we had nothing in common, nothing to say? Sentenced for an hour, across from each other, with nothing but a fork to twirl and cold food to stare at.

The relationship with Rebecca was starting to look surprisingly flawless. The good old days, when we would sit in a restaurant and whisper to each other, without pressures, without the fear of rejection.

I dipped my finger into my water glass and held it there, submerged in ice, as if the cold could somehow obstruct the passage of time. I wondered if Rebecca missed me, if the memories shadowed her as they did me. Rebecca, who would be anxious to dine with a woman like Marlo, whose only worry would be what name she would call out during sex.

"Been here long?" Marlo glanced first at my eyes then down to my finger still submerged in the ice water.

Casually stirring the water, I motioned to the seat next to me. "Just got here," I lied. For some reason, with Marlo, a small lie seemed reasonable.

Marlo flashed an amused smile. I was uncertain whether it was sincere or merely an acknowledgement that women tended to lie when they were with her.

She slipped into the chair. "I'm late," she said, her narrow eyes glinting, "because I stopped to get you these."

She pulled a handful of daisies from behind her.

I studied her cat-like eyes, her full lips that instinctively molded into a playful smirk. Entranced, I followed the angle of her short dark hair, spiked to a wild edge, as it grazed the raised collar of her white crisp shirt.

"So sweet of you," I finally managed. Marlo was more stunning than I had remembered.

Her steely eyes penetrated me and I was struck by the sudden need to look away. Yet I didn't move, didn't lower my eyes.

"I like daisies," Marlo said, as though revealing a guarded secret, "because they are so haphazard, so unpredictable."

"Unpredictable?" I said, transfixed by her elusive eyes.

"A troublesome weed," she said with an impish smile. "A troublesome weed that is a symbol of love's roulette."

She pulled one flower from the bunch and began plucking the petals. "Loves me, loves me not."

The petals sprinkled into my water glass and floated like tiny white canoes.

"Do you like the water?" I said, lost in thought. I lifted a pearl-shaded petal from the glass.

"I'd rather have some wine." Marlo reached for the wine list.

"No, I meant boating . . ."

I lie back in the canoe and listen to the peaceful sound of the water. The sun is hot and there are beads of sweat between my breasts. Even with the brim of the straw hat shading my eyes, I have to squint to see Marlo, who has removed her top, who has revealed her brown nipples.

The creases in my arms are lined with perspiration and there are trails of dampness between my thighs. I spread my legs and the cotton skirt hikes up.

Marlo looks down at me. "The heat suits you," she says.

It is difficult to know whether she is staring at my face or up the cotton skirt, the white cotton skirt that is damp with my sweat.

"I like the heat. I like the water," I say, my words melted and sticky from the sun.

Marlo scoops a palm full of water. I can hear ripples as she dips into it.

"The lake is cold." She dribbles the water between her breasts and across her nipples. "It feels good."

She scoops more water and leans into me. Her

body intrudes between myself and the sun, and suddenly I can see her clearly. Her nipples are tightened from the water, her flesh is alert from the cold. She drizzles the water onto my knees and it streams, like tiny rivers, down my legs.

The cold is quick and alarming. Her hands slide up my slippery thighs, beneath the white cotton skirt. I reach for her nipples. Like thick raisins, they are plump and ripe. I press them between my fingers. The tissue is firm yet pliable. I stretch them, pull on them, twist them carefully.

The look on Marlo's face is one I have never seen before. There is a wildness in her, waiting to be released.

"Come on, Marlo," I growl. "Come on and fuck me."

"I'd say that rafting trip was my last boating venture for a while!" Marlo chuckled.

Marlo's laugh pulled me back from my fantasy. In my glass, the white canoes floated peacefully in the water.

"I like the land, the mountains. After all, I'm a Scorpio," she said carelessly, flashing a speculative smile. "But beware, they say we sting."

I watched her as she spoke. The thing I savored most about Marlo was the very thing I disliked. She was so deliciously, deplorably sure of herself. Her mouth suggested sex and her gypsy eyes shifted with promises of adventure.

"Who's they?" I asked. I wondered how good her sting actually felt.

"The astrologers. But it doesn't matter, not really, because the sting implies a certain boldness. Boldness is attractive, magnetic." Marlo extended her hand toward me. "Grab on, if you dare."

I thought she was a little too arrogant for my liking. I grabbed her hand anyway. After all, I liked her arrogance.

I slip my hand into Marlo's and am hypnotized by the heat. Her hand is strong as it encloses mine, I can feel her power simmering. Her fingers are thick. A bold gold band encircles her index; three diamonds catch the light as she tightens her hand around mine.

She has my hand, a hapless hostage, and pulls it under the table, to her unzipped pants. I scan the restaurant. The diners are oblivious to our corner booth, our Greek salads abandoned and sifted through. No one takes note of the desperate hand pushed into the unzipped pants of my spiked-haired companion.

Marlo's pink tongue wets her lips then disappears. She smiles and her eyes narrow with intent. She says nothing, yet her eyes say it all.

She crushes my hand against her hard belly and hunger burns through me. I wonder if she'll get my hand to her hair, I wonder how far she can force my fingers between her snug pants and smooth belly.

I lean in, I want to tangle my fingers in her silk-soft sable. Her breath is hard and fire escapes her eyes. My heart races in a mad beat. I want it, I want it, I want it.

"Go ahead," she whispers, her voice throaty and hoarse. She arches her hips and plunges my hand through the plush fur and into her petaled flesh.

Her hand is tight against my forearm. My flesh stings from her twisted grasp. She jams my hand, stuffs my hand, into her sweet well and I am drowning in passion.

I can't move my fingers like I want to. I try to turn my hand, to dip into her juice. I ache to press her knotted clit between my fingers.

"Pull your pants down," I demand.

She lowers them, my hand dips into her delicious mystery and I am not disappointed. The flesh is soaked with sap and my fortunate fingers slip against her oily charms.

Building the heat, I stroke her, drive my fingers across her stiffness. Her eyes are sharp and thirsty as she begs me for more.

"Yes, baby, oh yes." She pants. She squirms. "Nice hands, sweet hands."

I pump her hard, I take her hard. She comes like thunder, comes like lightning.

"Oh yes, oh yes, oh yes!"

"Yes or no?" Marlo tapped me with the dessert menu. "Do you want dessert?"

My hand ached. I had twisted it precariously between my thighs and hadn't even noticed. The dessert I wanted was after paying the bill. How the hell do I get from the restaurant, I wondered, into the pants of delicious Marlo?

* * * * *

We went to the Detour in separate cars. Marlo
figured it would save us a drive back across town.
On the other hand, I wasn't in the mood for
time-saving shortcuts. Rebecca had told me that
timing is crucial in sexual matters. It was relatively
simple. I wanted a hot fling with Marlo, I wanted it
tonight, and with my lack of expertise in the
seduction department, I'd need every available
minute to reach my goal.

The Detour was packed, which was not unusual
for a Saturday night. What was unusual was the
first person I noticed when I walked into the
smoke-filled room. Rebecca.

Rebecca shot me a cool glance and whispered to
the platinum kewpie doll who was tucked under her
strong arm. The woman turned slightly and gave me
an off-handed glimpse.

I appraised the blonde quickly. She had
black-lined eyes and crimson-stained, pouty lips. A
black, oversized leather jacket with a Bela Lugosi
portrait airbrushed on the back hung loosely from
her shoulders.

How typical, I thought, irritated. Rebecca used to
talk about that type of woman. Rebels, she called
them, with bleached hair and coal black roots, dark
penciled eyes and powder-pale faces. Women that
lived life on the edge. "They like to be fucked,"
Rebecca said, "on car hoods and against rough brick
walls."

What annoyed me was my certainty that Rebecca
was already fucking her, God only knew in how
many crazy ways. I barely had the nerve to attempt

a good-night kiss with Marlo, let alone fuck her on my car.

"Parking's a bitch." Marlo's arrival caught my attention. She threw her arm around my shoulder in a gesture of suggested intimacy.

Yeah, look who's fucking *me*, I thought smugly. I hoped, though Rebecca had turned away, that she was watching me from the corner of her eye. After all, Marlo, with her rough-cut hair, her challenging eyes, looked like she'd fucked on many car hoods.

Marlo led me to the back of the bar, and I quickly lost interest in Rebecca and her rebel blonde. Instead I concentrated on Marlo.

Marlo's dancing was hypnotic. It was impossible to watch her and not think of lying under her, naked, in a feather-stuffed bed, or beneath her on a hardwood floor, or even slammed against a rough tree. She lunged, she thrust her hips, she pushed her arms. Her body insinuated serious pleasure with wordless motions. Her eyes, quick-shifting and dangerous, peered into mine with steamy intent.

This woman was sex — hot, ready. It was oozing all over her, oozing all over me. I'm going to get it tonight, I thought, my panties wet with desire. I imagined her, above me, her legs spread. What did she look like between those muscular legs? Like Rebecca, small and delicate? Like me, pulpy and thick? Would she like it hard? Could I do it hard enough, fast enough for her? What if I couldn't make her come? What if I did it all wrong?

"I think we should call it a night," Marlo said suddenly. She pulled me from the dance floor. "I've got an early day tomorrow."

Disappointment swirled around me. What did she

mean, "call it a night?" I fretted like a small child whose candy had been taken away. She had danced like we were going to fuck, she had smiled like sex was a certain conclusion.

She threw her arm around me, then she escorted me through the women and to my car. I was quiet, had nothing to say. I thought of Rebecca, probably out on a deserted road, with blondie propped on the front of a car, legs spread, crying out in the night.

"Can I call you?" Marlo asked as she hugged me. She touched her warm lips to mine. I thought of grabbing her hair, of smashing my lips into hers, of pushing her against my car hood and ramming my face between her legs.

I kissed her back, gently. My tongue lightly touched hers. "Yes, I'd like that," I murmured and climbed into the car.

I didn't want to go home. I knew exactly what would greet me there — a darkened room, an empty bed, a pillow to grab and a vibrator. I had promised myself there'd be no more of that.

I watched Marlo disappear around the corner and after a few minutes, I walked back into the Detour. It was one o'clock and the crowd was beginning to thin. I ordered a drink and scanned the faces.

"Come back for more?" A familiar voice teased my ear. I turned to see Rebecca sporting a playful smile.

"I thought we were fighting," I said.

"Ah, shit, Carla, so we can't make it as lovers. I see you across the room and think it's crazy to pretend like I don't know you." Rebecca flashed a seductive smile. "I *do* know you, don't I?"

I ignored the innuendo and glanced to the corner

where Rebecca's vampire blonde sat. Black-lensed sunglasses now shielded her eyes and I was unsure if she was watching us.

"That's Ricki," Rebecca said as though reading my mind. Rebecca knew me, that was certain.

I gave Rebecca a simple nod.

"Where's your friend?" Rebecca glanced around the room.

No fucking way I'm telling you her name, I thought defensively. A quick flash of Rebecca cruising Marlo whisked through my mind.

"Went home." I looked back to Ricki, who was sipping a drink, seemingly staring at us.

"Want to join us?" Rebecca inquired, all casual and friendly.

"What's up, Rebecca?" I asked suspiciously.

Rebecca leaned in close. "I'm looking out for you, that's all." She ran her thick finger across my neck. "So we can't be in a relationship. There's no reason to cut me out of your life completely, is there?"

I shrugged.

"No, I didn't think so," Rebecca's voice was hot whiskey and cream. "And Ricki," she motioned to the blonde, "wants to meet you."

"One of your rebel-girls?" I quipped.

"Car hoods and brick walls," she said with a wink.

I ended up crammed in the back seat of Ricki's sports car. We were cruising down Highway 1, top down, the chilled air cutting through me. I crouched close to the front, occasionally able to decipher wind-blown words from the conversation in the front seat.

The streaming wind fanned Ricki's hair from her pale, shaded face. The roots of her platinum hair were shadowed with darkness. Fucking rebel-girl, I thought, with a combination of bitterness and fascination.

I glanced at Rebecca, her arm slung carelessly across Ricki's shoulders. She had that look, her story look, as she leaned toward Ricki and whispered in her ear.

It's not that I was jealous of Ricki — she could have the fighting, she could have the turmoil. It was Rebecca's mystifying ability to score, her obvious talent to solicit an unending supply of women, that annoyed me.

I glanced at the sky. The full moon, a sudden victim to a curtain of clouds, was in rapid recovery. It slid out from beneath the black, and again the road became illuminated with a silver backdrop.

Ricki unexpectedly swerved to the side of the road and shut the engine off. Not bothering to open the door, she jumped over the side. Rebecca leaped from the car and hurried to Ricki who was standing, arms crossed, in the moonlight.

"What's your fucking problem?" Rebecca grabbed the front of Ricki's oversized leather jacket.

"Don't give me your bullshit." Blondie pushed at Rebecca. "You're the one with the fucking problem. You say meet Carla, I meet her. You say take her with us, we take her with us." Ricki motioned toward me. "Am I some kind of entertainment set-up for your ex?"

Rebecca pushed Ricki against the car hood. "Entertainment set-up?"

Oh shit, I thought, blinking hard. I break up with Rebecca and she offers me a chance to do a threesome argument. When it came to sex, I was having a severe run of bad luck.

"Hey, look," I said without thinking. "I thought we were out for a ride. What's the big deal, just take me back to the bar and I'll be fine."

Rebecca pulled me out of the car, over to Ricki. "I think you owe Carla an apology," Rebecca said harshly.

I shook my head. No apology was really needed.

Ricki shot me a cold look. "I'm not into charity sex."

What the fuck was that supposed to mean? As far as I was concerned, Rebecca was right. That fucking bitch owed me an apology.

"No?" Rebecca grabbed Ricki again.

"No," Ricki said stubbornly.

Did Ricki have any idea what Rebecca was like when provoked? Obviously not.

Jerking a fistful of her straw-white hair, Rebecca slammed Ricki onto the car hood.

"Rebecca, please." I tried to placate her.

Rebecca, in one quick movement, yanked Ricki's pants until they hung haphazardly from one slender ankle. Although Rebecca's flamboyant anger set me back, I had to admit I was impressed by her masterful, swift removal of Ricki's pants.

Ricki stopped arguing. Her bare ass was flush

against the cold car hood. There was a subtle smirk on her face as Rebecca slowly inched her back.

My eyes were drawn to her thick patch of jet-black sex hair, a severe contrast to her peroxide-blonde locks. A spider tattoo bordered the dark curls, as though a recent escapee from the tangled web — her fast-girl image, indelible pigment on her smooth belly. A rebel-girl all the way.

Black leather jacket, Bela Lugosi, pressed against the red hood, bleached-blonde hair swept against the windshield. The air was charged with a contagious electricity. I felt it. The telltale look in Rebecca's eyes indicated she felt it too. I glanced back to Ricki. Her black-lined eyes were wild with excitement. No doubt, the feeling was unanimous.

Rebecca spread Ricki's knees, and the black net hair parted. A torturous throbbing between my legs impelled me to inch toward the front of the car, slightly behind Rebecca. I had to see, first-hand, what was perched between the thick, dark, rebel-girl lips.

"Yeah, entertainment set-up, all right," Rebecca muttered.

Yeah, entertainment set-up, I thought.

"Yes, entertainment set-up," Ricki sighed.

We were in agreement. And what was even better, it looked as though I was going to be involved in some real live sex. No pillow, no fantasies, just Rebecca and me, taking a rebel-blonde on a car hood.

Rebecca pulled Ricki's pussy lips apart. The blazing moon cast a shimmering haze onto Ricki's ivory skin.

"Looks pale by the light of the moon, white skin

in this ace-of-spades hair," Rebecca said with a wicked smile. "Does this mean you're not aroused?"

Ricki shook her head and attempted to speak but Rebecca clamped her palm over Ricki's mouth. "You're usually red when you're hot. So what should we do, Ricki?"

Still muffled by Rebecca's hand, Ricki reached into her coat pocket. I saw a glint of gold as she passed something to Rebecca.

"That's a good girl," Rebecca said, her voice steamed.

She clamped the lips apart with one hand and she brought the golden object to her mouth with the other. Using her teeth, she pulled the top off the lipstick tube and spit it to the ground.

"Color it red for me, Carla," Rebecca insisted. She tossed the tube to me. "Color it nice and red for me."

Somehow, I had walked straight into the lead role of Rebecca's story. I was impossibly aroused. Rebecca was spreading out one of her fantasies like a fancy buffet. I twisted the lipstick. Even in the frosted moonlight, the lipstick glimmered red.

I smoothed the tip of the lip cream into the pulled-flat folds of pussy flesh. The skin seemed to suck in the color. I sliced the tube up one side and down another. All the while, I was mesmerized by the thickened center flap. Leaving a trail of glossy brick-red against the moon-blanched skin, I continued to paint the tissue.

I followed the natural slope down into the creased slit and circled the lipstick around the darkened opening. I rimmed the raised edges with red lip paint.

I glanced at Ricki's face. The same color stained her lips, those Kewpie-doll lips. I appraised that cheap, "blonde-my-ass" hair; those penciled "I like to be fucked" eyes; the collar of the black leather jacket raised around the ready-to-be-sucked neck. Jesus Christ, this was a dream come true.

I rammed the lipstick into her slit. Pushed it, in and out — red on the little lips, red on the ace-of-spades hair, red on the base of my hands, my sticky wet fingers. Lip cream, pussy cream, everything was glossy wet. I had dropped the tube, or had I? I didn't give a fuck where it was. My fingers went in, slid in, sunk into the wet, rebel-girl's, bad girl's, "I-want-it-hard" girl's sweet snatch.

Rebecca's word, "snatch." Behind me, Rebecca whispered, "Yeah, in her snatch, in her snatch."

I never liked that word — male, street corner, cat-call word. But at that moment, *snatch* was the word, the perfect word; for where my hand had found refuge was definitely a hot snatch. Soaked fingers, I pumped her hard, fucked her with one, then two, then three, then four.

"Fist me," she gasped as Rebecca squirted the lube.

And Rebecca had told me stories about that — fisting women — but I couldn't seem to take that final plunge. I was scared. So instead I stuck two fingers from one hand in, two from the other at the same time and rammed them, in and out, alternating.

Never did that before, and that's the thing about hot sex, you find yourself creating all kinds of motions. And I was moving my hands so fast, like I was going to start a fire, and everything was red, and the vampire let out a scream and I was out of my mind, hot, and Rebecca slammed her hands up under my shirt, squeezed my nipples so hard that I screamed too . . .

And that was my first time with a rebel-girl, and later that night, in bed, I didn't feel so bad about Marlo leaving me stranded.

"I've only been out of a relationship for three months," Marlo said, contemplating a honeybee as it boldly investigated her glass of wine. "So I've decided to take some time, try to get to know myself."

"Same with me," I said definitively. I watched three ducks lazily paddle their way across the lake. I was pleased that Marlo had asked me to lunch, pleased that we had come to this lake.

An untied ribbon spilled a bouquet of spring flowers precariously close to the array of fruits, cheeses, rolls and wine that Marlo had pulled from her thick woven basket. Spread across a quilted blanket, the contrasting colors created a watercolor ambience.

"I'm not looking to fall in love," Marlo said. She stared ahead, unblinking.

"Then we should get along just fine." I glanced absently toward the lake. "That's the last thing I'm looking for."

After all, I thought as I contemplated the ducks, since the other night's incident with Rebecca and the blonde, I had a new, mint-condition, self-confidence. I was hot, I was unstoppable. The door had opened to the sexy, lesbian single world. Rebel-girls and Rebecca, women like Marlo, the spiked-haired checker at the grocery store — yeah, I could have these women and anyone else I damn well wanted.

Marlo didn't want to fall in love and neither did I. I had illusions of the next few months, a shining world of women unfolding in my life. Sex would be delicious, variety the spice.

Marlo brushed her lips against my cheek in a teasing kiss. Overwhelmed with my new-found assertiveness, I guided her lips to mine and kissed her.

As my tongue lightly skimmed Marlo's lips, I solicited an invitation to push further. Marlo's thick lips acknowledged the request and slowly separated. My tongue pressed into Marlo's warm mouth.

Grabbing me in a bold embrace, Marlo pushed me down onto the blanket. Amid the spring flowers, the yellow and white cheeses, the sweet French rolls, the empty bottle of red wine, we capsized.

Climbing between my legs, Marlo rocked back and forth. The distinct hardness of her prominent mound pressed against mine and her expert way of rotating her hips created a scarlet heat within my damp folds.

"You like this?" Marlo whispered in a husky voice. "You like how I feel?"

I clamped my fingers into the thin material of Marlo's T-shirt, desperate to keep the slapping sensation of Marlo's hardness against my ravenous cunt. I could barely speak, what with the slamming, what with the rough thumping between my legs.

Marlo kissed me, a deep kiss, a hungry kiss. She penetrated into my hot mouth repeatedly, her tongue searching the slippery tissues. Pushing her hands against my pink tank-top, she roughly pressed my palm-sized breasts.

Moaning, I struggled to lift my hips as best I could, to hang on as Marlo rode me. Marlo could move. Marlo could work her hips. Marlo was driving her thick prominence, over and over, against my jeans, against the flesh that housed my sweet aching clit.

"Let me take my pants down," I said hurriedly. "Take yours down. C'mon, Marlo, c'mon."

Marlo lifted slightly, still churning her hips. "No, we keep our clothes on," Marlo panted, her lips slick with a nasty smile. Control glistened in her eyes.

Continuing to buck, Marlo moved in a rhythm. She rotated, bounced, jammed, humped.

"Marlo, Marlo, Marlo!" Stunned that it could feel so good, that she could hit me so right, I tossed, I whirled. "Never like this, never like this!" I cried.

And it was true. I had never been completely dressed and been so hot, so close to climax. Marlo hadn't touched my nipples, hadn't stroked my hardened clit. Yet, I was ready. My entire body was fired, ready to launch. Hips thrusting hips, mound slamming mound, hands tangling into perfumed hair, breasts rubbing breasts, we pushed into each other. I grabbed Marlo's shoulders.

"I want more," I pleaded. "I want to touch you, feel you touch me."

Marlo rolled to her side. "I want you too."

I reached for the brass button on Marlo's jeans but my hand was quickly detoured by Marlo. "Why are you stopping me?" I asked, confused.

"Because I want you slow, a little at a time. Our clothes on, just rubbing each other. Tell me it wasn't hot, tell me you aren't crazy for more." Marlo traced my earlobe with her finger. "Nothing is hotter than anticipation. One step at a time till the time is right."

"And how do we know when the time is right?" I asked skeptically.

Marlo smiled, her nasty smile, that controlling smile, that young Brando, "you-got-to-trust-me" Scorpion smile. "Oh, don't you worry about that. We'll just know."

"What's not to get?" Rebecca said as she checked her reflection in my hall mirror. She lifted the collar of her jean jacket to create the "butch on call" look she preferred.

I watched her shift to get a better view of her profile. With the amount of weight she lifted, she had sculpted her ass to perfection.

"I guess there is something to anticipation, but I'm not sure what the point is." I was still deliberating Marlo's idea to go slow.

"The point is . . ." Rebecca turned from the mirror.

Dressed in my tan shorts and a beige halter top, I could feel her eyes devour me as though I were a gingersnap cookie sprinkled with sugar. Rebecca licked her lips and I suspected her sweet tooth ached unbearably.

"I know," I said, turning away. "The point is how hot it's going to be when she's finally in my pants."

"Yeah," Rebecca smirked. She turned me, shoving me against the wall.

I was in a state of constant anticipation. Rebecca probably read it in my eyes, saw it scribbled across my tight-nippled breasts. She knew me all right. It was just like Rebecca to take advantage of a situation.

"So while you wait for her . . . ?" Rebecca's voice tingled with promise. Did she imagine her hands down my sugar-cookie shorts?

The coolness of the wall was against my back. One knot secured my halter top. One knot separated my breasts from Rebecca's strong fingers.

I was smitten by the fragrance of Lancome that swirled through Rebecca's dark hair. Her scent beckoned me to step closer, to perhaps untie that knot myself. If Marlo thought we should wait — and her suggestion did have unquestionable appeal, an intriguing element to it — well, more power to her.

But in the meantime, Rebecca, all cologne and come-on hands, offered her brand of eroticism — hot, hard and immediate. Rebecca meant now. As for anticipation, I'd save that for Marlo.

Without another thought, I untied the knot and opened my lips to kiss Rebecca.

* * * * *

160

Marlo fascinated me. We sat in the movie theater, her arm carelessly tucked into mine, and I had difficulty concentrating on the film. She was right. Anticipation was definitely hot. All I could think of was how her body had felt pressed against mine, how it would feel when we lay together naked, her fingers searching for my swollen clit.

On the blanket, under the sun, Marlo had entranced me. She was like curry, a mysterious spice. She was fresh pepper, hot and biting. Her mocha eyes sparkled with heated messages. Marlo knew what she wanted and how to get there.

"You got to trust me." The innuendo behind Marlo's challenging words still enticed me. I glanced at her as she watched the movie. She seemed oblivious, as though she had escaped into the silver screen's unending world.

I marveled that she could sit, her arm entwined in mine, and not be struck by the insistent heat. I certainly felt it. There was a churning, almost a boiling quality, to it.

Perhaps she felt the excitement, yet had mysteriously cloaked it beneath her sultry demeanor. I wasn't sure. The way she stared ahead offered no clues.

"Like it?" Marlo turned to me with a whisper. Was she referring to the movie or the heightened tension of anticipation?

"Very much." I squeezed her hand in mine.

"I thought you would." Her words were sly and inviting. In the dim light, a provocative smile teased her full lips. In that brief moment, in her smoky smile, my question had been answered. Anticipation, like lightly flicking, thick fingers, was definitely hot.

After the movie, after a few dances at the Detour, Marlo drove me home. I had sweet visions of grabbing Marlo's ass tucked snugly in her tight black jeans and pulling her against me. I would spread my legs, I would dip my tongue into her hot mouth. She knew what I wanted. It was written all over her face. How her smile tantalized me! How her eyes lured!

We would lie on my couch with Marlo on top of me like before, at the picnic. With those rough jeans stretched across her prominent pelvic bone, her tank top flaunting her rigid dark nipples, she would rub me, grind me into orgasm.

"Would you like to come in for coffee?" I asked flirtatiously as I opened the car door.

Marlo hesitated, ran her fingers through her spiked hair, then pulled me back into the car. "Is it really coffee you're offering?"

I shook my head. Who was I kidding? I didn't drink coffee, never have had a cup of coffee, didn't even have any in the house.

"Then what are you saying?" Marlo's words slurred with the touch of her fingers on my neck.

"I want you on top of me, like before," I said, the fire building between my thighs.

"You liked that?" Marlo asked teasingly.

Enough small talk, I thought. I pushed my fingers into Marlo's spiked hair. I figured I could take chances now, after all, what did I have to lose? From famine to feast, my sexual future had recently brightened. There were women, plenty of women.

There was Rebecca, who had pushed me against

the wall and forced her fingers down my shorts. She had pumped me like fire, lifted me, pushed me against the cold wall and brought me to trembling climax. The fierceness in her eyes, the sense of immediacy in her quickened breath, the fact that I was still hot from the anticipation with Marlo, all intermingled to make the sex incredibly hot.

There was Ricki, whose cheap blonde hair and black leather jacket created an aura of trespass. Sex with her evoked a distinct edge. I had stepped into territory where I didn't belong. On a car hood, on a fucking car hood, I slammed her like I had done it a hundred times. And in that moment, I felt like I had, indeed, fucked many women on countless car hoods.

There was Marlo, who was hot pepper, intoxicating coriander and cumin. She climbed on me, moved on me, kneaded into me.

Yeah, I had earned the right to take chances, to ask for what I wanted. I pressed my lips to Marlo's and scrambled toward her. I opened her shirt, I didn't care. I lifted her tank top, I didn't care. I squeezed her pert nipples, I didn't care.

Thinking of the hot sun, thinking of those rough jeans, I sucked her nipple into my mouth, smashed her breasts against my face. I wanted it, like before, and I didn't care.

Did Marlo let out a moan? A laugh? It was muffled and indistinct. My skirt was hiked to my thighs and her black jeans blotted my saturated panties. She lifted her knee, raised her leg. I could feel the pressure against my soaked flesh and rammed against her.

Marlo lifted me, pushed me to the passenger

seat. With her palm, she rubbed, again, across my thin panties. The silk crotch was slick with juice. In circles, back and forth, she pushed, then slapped, her strong palm.

I could smell sex, could hear the slippery noises. I wanted her to pull my panties aside. I could barely stand it. I grabbed to help, to rip the panties out of her way, out of our way.

Marlo suddenly stopped. "Coffee sounds great."

"Are you crazy?" My voice was reckless, my body ached.

"Yes." Marlo's breath was short. "Crazy for you."

Crazy for me. So crazy that she started her car, drove to a small cafe on the outskirts of San Francisco, and bought me an espresso. I didn't have the nerve to tell her I didn't drink coffee. I sipped the dark liquid as if I had done it all my life.

Marlo was enjoying an almond-swirled pastry. Her fingers pulled the pastry into pieces with unintentional gestures of passion. With each sip of coffee, her eyes yielded a sultry half-squint, her tongue occasionally slicing across her coffee-flavored lips. Every movement she made, no matter how subtle, was enhanced by a sensual undertone.

Marlo's fingers, dark and thick, contrasted with the delicate powdered sugar that coated her almond croissant. She swirled a thin film of sugar onto her finger and brought it to her lips. Sipping my coffee, I imagined those same fingers iced with my white cream, sticky and sweet.

"It's almost two." Marlo glanced at her wristwatch. "I should get you home."

"Will you spend the night?" I was trying to appear relaxed, although an unruly energy buzzed through me. My fingers drummed restlessly on my thigh and a rebellious twitch graced my right eyelid.

"Could we sleep together and not have sex?" Marlo asked.

I was uncertain if this was a statement or a dare. It didn't matter. I couldn't fathom sitting in the cafe much longer, what with the sudden urge to tap my foot.

"Sure." I stood up. "No sex." These things were always negotiable, I thought impetuously. Hadn't Rebecca said so?

I glanced at my espresso cup which, to my surprise, was empty. I remembered sipping, but not actually drinking, the bitter brew. Yet as the vacant cup stared back at me, I was aware of a biting vitality, a zip, surging through my body. I could hear the subtle beat of my heart, dull yet insistent, in my ears. No big deal. When I got Marlo in bed, I'd be grateful for the extra energy.

Marlo flailed herself across my bed. "I'm exhausted," she groaned as she worked her boot off with her foot.

Watching her reflection in the mirror, I marveled that she could be tired. I rinsed my face, brushed my teeth then looked over to her again. She was already asleep, tight jeans and all.

Grateful for the extra energy! I was disappointed. I gave Marlo a slight shove, partly to make room for myself, partly to stir her. She didn't respond, so I sat wide awake and watched Marlo sleep blissfully.

Marlo looked surprisingly open and vulnerable as

she slept. I ran my hand gently through her hair, across her soft cheek and was unexpectedly consumed with a sense of caring, of intimacy. I kissed her forehead lightly.

My thoughts drifted to Rebecca. A cold vacant sensation passed through me. Our recent sexual adventures seemed suddenly dismal and empty. It was moments like this, enveloped in a haze of tenderness, that I really wanted. Taking time, getting to know someone, like Marlo and I had.

I recalled the way we had talked over coffee, the sweetness of her kiss, the strength in her eyes. Here was a woman I could fall in love with.

It was Marlo, with her tough-boy looks, her sexy demeanor, her Scorpion attitude that held my fancy. I considered how I would approach her with my newfound feelings. I had a certain sense about things and as I appraised the look of contentment on her face, I suspected that Marlo's feelings had shifted also.

Thinking of Marlo, engulfed in my feelings for her, I encircled her in my arms and drifted into sleep.

We are drifting on a lake. Marlo turns to me with a smile. The love she has for me fills me with a sudden warmth. Rebecca waves from the shore. She is naked and is surrounded by beautiful women but I only want Marlo. I turn to Marlo who kisses me.

The canoe rocks gently as Marlo's tender touch lifts me toward the clouds. Her caress is mesmerizing. There is nothing but Marlo. She kisses my hair, my cheeks, my neck, and we float, we soar. I am swept into Marlo, captive to her sweet kisses.

166

She is warm from the sun and I am consumed by desire. I press my lips to steal her heat, to absorb her magic into my mouth. She moans softly as I lovingly taste her brown-sugared skin. Little bites, gentle licks — I kiss my way down her neck, across her shoulder, to her breasts. Her nipples are puckered with anticipation. Like ripened berries, dark with juice, they perch dramatically.

I encircle a blackberry nipple and take it into my mouth. Her succulent flesh is firm yet pliable and I roll it carefully with my tongue.

"So sweet," Marlo says.

My fingers pluck and pull the other thick nipple.

"Carla, yes."

I take both nipples into my mouth at once. I suck, gently at first, teasing the nipples with simultaneous tongue-play. Marlo whispers but I have lost track of her words. I can only hear the suction sound as I draw off, as I lovingly pump her cherry-hard nipples.

Marlo cries out. I know she is pleased. I suck, then drag the stiff and engorged nipples between my lightly clenched teeth.

I whirl in a berry patch of deep reds, dark purples, and divinely black-blues. Her nipples are swollen, thick. I hold her breasts together, rub her nipples against each other in my mouth.

Marlo grabs my hair as she shudders into deep pleasure. "Don't stop," she cries.

And I don't. I make her come. I please her beyond reason.

"I love you so much," she murmurs.

"I love you, too."

* * * * *

Marlo's slight nudge brought me out of my dream.

"I've changed my mind," she murmured. She kissed me lightly on the lips.

I felt momentarily disoriented. Had she been watching me sleep? Had she reached the same conclusions as I? Had she changed her mind about falling in love?

"You have?" I said softly. This is it, this is it, I thought.

Marlo did not hesitate. She pushed her hand under my oversized T-shirt and pulled me on top of her. Her hands were strong. Her hands were single-minded. Ripping at my T-shirt, she knew what she wanted, without compromise.

My passion spiraled like summer heat. Her hands moved over me in undisputed ownership. Her thick fingers searched between my dampened flesh and I wrapped my arms around her, kissing her like crazy. Opening me, she pried her fingers into wetness.

"Oh yeah," she moaned. She had one hand on my shoulder, the other thrust into me.

She took me fast. Anticipation had been thrown to the wind. She was fire, she was white heat. She pumped me like I was putty, like there was no end.

I squirmed, I shuddered. Digging my fingers into her back, I cried out. My body swirled in crimson hues as she plunged into me unrelentingly.

I came like hard thunder, flash floods, tropical storms. I tightened, then arched as I held on for life.

When I hit the end, swept in delirious pleasure, I grabbed onto Marlo.

It was faster than I had expected it. It was harder. But we'd have time, plenty of time for tenderness in the future, I thought as I silently drifted.

"When I woke up in your arms," Marlo said, her voice breaking the quiet, "you were so soft, so vulnerable. I couldn't wait any longer." She sat up with a laugh. "Funny how we can change our minds without notice. Last night I wanted anticipation and this morning, all I could think of was sex."

I felt a bolt hit my heart. Her words seemed so callous, so detached.

"That's what you changed your mind about?" I whispered. A tear leaped over my lashes and pushed down my cheek, followed by another.

Marlo glanced nervously at my tears. "Isn't that what you wanted?"

I didn't reply. My throat was suddenly parched.

"You okay?" Marlo shifted as though uncomfortable.

There was a subtle distance in her voice, a thinly disguised coldness in her eyes. She had the air of a scorpion moments before its defensive sting.

I wiped my tears. "I'm fine . . . really."

At one time, I had fantasized that her sting might feel good. Now I realized the Scorpion's pit was no refuge for the open-hearted.

She glanced quickly at the clock. "It's later than I thought," she said as if she were already gone.

I nodded.

"I'll call you." I heard the lie.

"Yes, good," I said. With a woman like her, a small lie seemed reasonable.

It's been a month since Marlo, since Ricki, since Rebecca. I'm much wiser and more experienced now. There are women, lots of women, and I do whatever I please. The possibilities are endless.

I have sex with strangers, sex with rebels, hot sex, cheap sex, fast sex, nasty sex. At night, in my bed, wrapped in the safety of my illusions, I am a wild tigress on the prowl.

COSTA BRAVA by Marta Balletbo Coll. 144 pp. Read the book, see the movie!   ISBN 1-56280-153-8 $11.95

MEETING MAGDALENE & OTHER STORIES by Marilyn Freeman. 160 pp. Read the book, see the movie!   ISBN 1-56280-170-8   11.95

SECOND FIDDLE by Kate Calloway. 240 pp. P.I. Cassidy James' second case.   ISBN 1-56280-169-6   11.95

LAUREL by Isabel Miller. 128 pp. By the author of the beloved *Patience and Sarah.*   ISBN 1-56280-146-5   10.95

LOVE OR MONEY by Jackie Calhoun. 240 pp. The romance of real life.   ISBN 1-56280-147-3   10.95

SMOKE AND MIRRORS by Pat Welch. 224 pp. 5th Helen Black Mystery.   ISBN 1-56280-143-0   10.95

DANCING IN THE DARK edited by Barbara Grier & Christine Cassidy. 272 pp. Erotic love stories by Naiad Press authors.   ISBN 1-56280-144-9   14.95

TIME AND TIME AGAIN by Catherine Ennis. 176 pp. Passionate love affair.   ISBN 1-56280-145-7   10.95

PAXTON COURT by Diane Salvatore. 256 pp. Erotic and wickedly funny contemporary tale about the business of learning to live together.   ISBN 1-56280-114-7   10.95

INNER CIRCLE by Claire McNab. 208 pp. 8th Carol Ashton Mystery.   ISBN 1-56280-135-X   10.95

LESBIAN SEX: AN ORAL HISTORY by Susan Johnson. 240 pp. Need we say more?   ISBN 1-56280-142-2   14.95

BABY, IT'S COLD by Jaye Maiman. 256 pp. 5th Robin Miller Mystery.   ISBN 1-56280-141-4   19.95

WILD THINGS by Karin Kallmaker. 240 pp. By the undisputed mistress of lesbian romance.   ISBN 1-56280-139-2   10.95

THE GIRL NEXT DOOR by Mindy Kaplan. 208 pp. Just what you'd expect. ISBN 1-56280-140-6   10.95

NOW AND THEN by Penny Hayes. 240 pp. Romance on the westward journey. ISBN 1-56280-121-X   10.95

HEART ON FIRE by Diana Simmonds. 176 pp. The romantic and erotic rival of *Curious Wine*. ISBN 1-56280-152-X   10.95

DEATH AT LAVENDER BAY by Lauren Wright Douglas. 208 pp. 1st Allison O'Neil Mystery. ISBN 1-56280-085-X   10.95

YES I SAID YES I WILL by Judith McDaniel. 272 pp. Hot romance by famous author. ISBN 1-56280-138-4   10.95

FORBIDDEN FIRES by Margaret C. Anderson. Edited by Mathilda Hills. 176 pp. Famous author's "unpublished" Lesbian romance. ISBN 1-56280-123-6   21.95

SIDE TRACKS by Teresa Stores. 160 pp. Gender-bending Lesbians on the road. ISBN 1-56280-122-8   10.95

HOODED MURDER by Annette Van Dyke. 176 pp. 1st Jessie Batelle Mystery. ISBN 1-56280-134-1   10.95

WILDWOOD FLOWERS by Julia Watts. 208 pp. Hilarious and heart-warming tale of true love. ISBN 1-56280-127-9   10.95

NEVER SAY NEVER by Linda Hill. 224 pp. Rule #1: Never get involved with . . . ISBN 1-56280-126-0   10.95

THE SEARCH by Melanie McAllester. 240 pp. Exciting top cop Tenny Mendoza case. ISBN 1-56280-150-3   10.95

THE WISH LIST by Saxon Bennett. 192 pp. Romance through the years. ISBN 1-56280-125-2   10.95

FIRST IMPRESSIONS by Kate Calloway. 208 pp. P.I. Cassidy James' first case. ISBN 1-56280-133-3   10.95

OUT OF THE NIGHT by Kris Bruyer. 192 pp. Spine-tingling thriller. ISBN 1-56280-120-1   10.95

NORTHERN BLUE by Tracey Richardson. 224 pp. Police recruits Miki & Miranda — passion in the line of fire. ISBN 1-56280-118-X   10.95

LOVE'S HARVEST by Peggy J. Herring. 176 pp. by the author of *Once More With Feeling*. ISBN 1-56280-117-1   10.95

THE COLOR OF WINTER by Lisa Shapiro. 208 pp. Romantic love beyond your wildest dreams. ISBN 1-56280-116-3   10.95

FAMILY SECRETS by Laura DeHart Young. 208 pp. Enthralling romance and suspense. ISBN 1-56280-119-8   10.95

INLAND PASSAGE by Jane Rule. 288 pp. Tales exploring conventional & unconventional relationships. ISBN 0-930044-56-8   10.95

DOUBLE BLUFF by Claire McNab. 208 pp. 7th Carol Ashton Mystery. ISBN 1-56280-096-5   10.95

BAR GIRLS by Lauran Hoffman. 176 pp. See the movie, read
the book!   ISBN 1-56280-115-5   10.95

THE FIRST TIME EVER edited by Barbara Grier & Christine
Cassidy. 272 pp. Love stories by Naiad Press authors.
                                               ISBN 1-56280-086-8   14.95

MISS PETTIBONE AND MISS McGRAW by Brenda Weathers.
208 pp. A charming ghostly love story.   ISBN 1-56280-151-1   10.95

CHANGES by Jackie Calhoun. 208 pp. Involved romance and
relationships.   ISBN 1-56280-083-3   10.95

FAIR PLAY by Rose Beecham. 256 pp. 3rd Amanda Valentine
Mystery.   ISBN 1-56280-081-7   10.95

PAYBACK by Celia Cohen. 176 pp. A gripping thriller of romance,
revenge and betrayal.   ISBN 1-56280-084-1   10.95

THE BEACH AFFAIR by Barbara Johnson. 224 pp. Sizzling
summer romance/mystery/intrigue.   ISBN 1-56280-090-6   10.95

GETTING THERE by Robbi Sommers. 192 pp. Nobody does it
like Robbi!   ISBN 1-56280-099-X   10.95

FINAL CUT by Lisa Haddock. 208 pp. 2nd Carmen Ramirez
Mystery.   ISBN 1-56280-088-4   10.95

FLASHPOINT by Katherine V. Forrest. 256 pp. A Lesbian
blockbuster!   ISBN 1-56280-079-5   10.95

CLAIRE OF THE MOON by Nicole Conn. Audio Book —Read
by Marianne Hyatt.   ISBN 1-56280-113-9   16.95

FOR LOVE AND FOR LIFE: INTIMATE PORTRAITS OF
LESBIAN COUPLES by Susan Johnson. 224 pp.
                                               ISBN 1-56280-091-4   14.95

DEVOTION by Mindy Kaplan. 192 pp. See the movie — read
the book!   ISBN 1-56280-093-0   10.95

SOMEONE TO WATCH by Jaye Maiman. 272 pp. 4th Robin
Miller Mystery.   ISBN 1-56280-095-7   10.95

GREENER THAN GRASS by Jennifer Fulton. 208 pp. A young
woman — a stranger in her bed.   ISBN 1-56280-092-2   10.95

TRAVELS WITH DIANA HUNTER by Regine Sands. Erotic
lesbian romp. Audio Book (2 cassettes)   ISBN 1-56280-107-4   16.95

CABIN FEVER by Carol Schmidt. 256 pp. Sizzling suspense
and passion.   ISBN 1-56280-089-1   10.95

THERE WILL BE NO GOODBYES by Laura DeHart Young. 192
pp. Romantic love, strength, and friendship.   ISBN 1-56280-103-1   10.95

FAULTLINE by Sheila Ortiz Taylor. 144 pp. Joyous comic
lesbian novel.   ISBN 1-56280-108-2   9.95

OPEN HOUSE by Pat Welch. 176 pp. 4th Helen Black Mystery.
                                               ISBN 1-56280-102-3   10.95

SMOKEY O by Celia Cohen. 176 pp. Relationships on the
playing field.   ISBN 1-56280-057-4   9.95

KATHLEEN O'DONALD by Penny Hayes. 256 pp. Rose and
Kathleen find each other and employment in 1909 NYC.
                                                  ISBN 1-56280-070-1   9.95

STAYING HOME by Elisabeth Nonas. 256 pp. Molly and Alix
want a baby . . . or do they?   ISBN 1-56280-076-0   10.95

TRUE LOVE by Jennifer Fulton. 240 pp. Six lesbians searching
for love in all the "right" places.   ISBN 1-56280-035-3   10.95

KEEPING SECRETS by Penny Mickelbury. 208 pp. 1st Gianna
Maglione Mystery.   ISBN 1-56280-052-3   9.95

THE ROMANTIC NAIAD edited by Katherine V. Forrest &
Barbara Grier. 336 pp. Love stories by Naiad Press authors.
                                     ISBN 1-56280-054-X   14.95

UNDER MY SKIN by Jaye Maiman. 336 pp. 3rd Robin Miller
Mystery.   ISBN 1-56280-049-3.   10.95

CAR POOL by Karin Kallmaker. 272pp. Lesbians on wheels
and then some!   ISBN 1-56280-048-5   10.95

NOT TELLING MOTHER: STORIES FROM A LIFE by Diane
Salvatore. 176 pp. Her 3rd novel.   ISBN 1-56280-044-2   9.95

GOBLIN MARKET by Lauren Wright Douglas. 240pp. 5th Caitlin
Reece Mystery.   ISBN 1-56280-047-7   10.95

LONG GOODBYES by Nikki Baker. 256 pp. 3rd Virginia Kelly
Mystery.   ISBN 1-56280-042-6   9.95

FRIENDS AND LOVERS by Jackie Calhoun. 224 pp. Mid-
western Lesbian lives and loves.   ISBN 1-56280-041-8   10.95

THE CAT CAME BACK by Hilary Mullins. 208 pp. Highly
praised Lesbian novel.   ISBN 1-56280-040-X   9.95

BEHIND CLOSED DOORS by Robbi Sommers. 192 pp. Hot,
erotic short stories.   ISBN 1-56280-039-6   9.95

CLAIRE OF THE MOON by Nicole Conn. 192 pp. See the
movie — read the book!   ISBN 1-56280-038-8   10.95

SILENT HEART by Claire McNab. 192 pp. Exotic Lesbian
romance.   ISBN 1-56280-036-1   10.95

THE SPY IN QUESTION by Amanda Kyle Williams. 256 pp.
4th Madison McGuire Mystery.   ISBN 1-56280-037-X   9.95

SAVING GRACE by Jennifer Fulton. 240 pp. Adventure and
romantic entanglement.   ISBN 1-56280-051-5   10.95

CURIOUS WINE by Katherine V. Forrest. 176 pp. Tenth Anniver-
sary Edition. The most popular contemporary Lesbian love story.
                                     ISBN 1-56280-053-1   10.95
    Audio Book (2 cassettes)   ISBN 1-56280-105-8   16.95

CHAUTAUQUA by Catherine Ennis. 192 pp. Exciting, romantic
adventure.   ISBN 1-56280-032-9   9.95

A PROPER BURIAL by Pat Welch. 192 pp. 3rd Helen Black
Mystery.   ISBN 1-56280-033-7   9.95

SILVERLAKE HEAT: A Novel of Suspense by Carol Schmidt.
240 pp. Rhonda is as hot as Laney's dreams.   ISBN 1-56280-031-0   9.95

LOVE, ZENA BETH by Diane Salvatore. 224 pp. The most talked
about lesbian novel of the nineties!   ISBN 1-56280-030-2   10.95

A DOORYARD FULL OF FLOWERS by Isabel Miller. 160 pp.
Stories incl. 2 sequels to *Patience and Sarah*. ISBN 1-56280-029-9   9.95

MURDER BY TRADITION by Katherine V. Forrest. 288 pp. 4th
Kate Delafield Mystery.   ISBN 1-56280-002-7   11.95

THE EROTIC NAIAD edited by Katherine V. Forrest & Barbara
Grier. 224 pp. Love stories by Naiad Press authors.
                                              ISBN 1-56280-026-4   14.95

DEAD CERTAIN by Claire McNab. 224 pp. 5th Carol Ashton
Mystery.   ISBN 1-56280-027-2   10.95

CRAZY FOR LOVING by Jaye Maiman. 320 pp. 2nd Robin Miller
Mystery.   ISBN 1-56280-025-6   10.95

STONEHURST by Barbara Johnson. 176 pp. Passionate regency
romance.   ISBN 1-56280-024-8   9.95

INTRODUCING AMANDA VALENTINE by Rose Beecham.
256 pp. 1st Amanda Valentine Mystery.   ISBN 1-56280-021-3   10.95

UNCERTAIN COMPANIONS by Robbi Sommers. 204 pp.
Steamy, erotic novel.   ISBN 1-56280-017-5   9.95

A TIGER'S HEART by Lauren W. Douglas. 240 pp. 4th Caitlin
Reece Mystery.   ISBN 1-56280-018-3   9.95

PAPERBACK ROMANCE by Karin Kallmaker. 256 pp. A
delicious romance.   ISBN 1-56280-019-1   10.95

THE LAVENDER HOUSE MURDER by Nikki Baker. 224 pp.
2nd Virginia Kelly Mystery.   ISBN 1-56280-012-4   9.95

PASSION BAY by Jennifer Fulton. 224 pp. Passionate romance,
virgin beaches, tropical skies.   ISBN 1-56280-028-0   10.95

STICKS AND STONES by Jackie Calhoun. 208 pp. Contemporary
lesbian lives and loves.   ISBN 1-56280-020-5   9.95
Audio Book (2 cassettes)   ISBN 1-56280-106-6   16.95

UNDER THE SOUTHERN CROSS by Claire McNab. 192 pp.
Romantic nights Down Under.   ISBN 1-56280-011-6   9.95

GRASSY FLATS by Penny Hayes. 256 pp. Lesbian romance in
the '30s.   ISBN 1-56280-010-8   9.95

A SINGULAR SPY by Amanda K. Williams. 192 pp. 3rd
Madison McGuire Mystery.   ISBN 1-56280-008-6   8.95

THE END OF APRIL by Penny Sumner. 240 pp. 1st Victoria
Cross Mystery.   ISBN 1-56280-007-8   8.95

KISS AND TELL by Robbi Sommers. 192 pp. Scorching stories
by the author of *Pleasures*.   ISBN 1-56280-005-1   10.95

STILL WATERS by Pat Welch. 208 pp. 2nd Helen Black Mystery.
                                        ISBN 0-941483-97-5   9.95

TO LOVE AGAIN by Evelyn Kennedy. 208 pp. Wildly romantic
love story.   ISBN 0-941483-85-1   9.95

IN THE GAME by Nikki Baker. 192 pp. 1st Virginia Kelly
Mystery.   ISBN 1-56280-004-3   9.95

STRANDED by Camarin Grae. 320 pp. Entertaining, riveting
adventure.   ISBN 0-941483-99-1   9.95

THE DAUGHTERS OF ARTEMIS by Lauren Wright Douglas.
240 pp. 3rd Caitlin Reece Mystery.   ISBN 0-941483-95-9   9.95

CLEARWATER by Catherine Ennis. 176 pp. Romantic secrets
of a small Louisiana town.   ISBN 0-941483-65-7   8.95

THE HALLELUJAH MURDERS by Dorothy Tell. 176 pp. 2nd
Poppy Dillworth Mystery.   ISBN 0-941483-88-6   8.95

SECOND CHANCE by Jackie Calhoun. 256 pp. Contemporary
Lesbian lives and loves.   ISBN 0-941483-93-2   9.95

BENEDICTION by Diane Salvatore. 272 pp. Striking, contemporary romantic novel.   ISBN 0-941483-90-8   10.95

TOUCHWOOD by Karin Kallmaker. 240 pp. Loving, May/
December romance.   ISBN 0-941483-76-2   9.95

COP OUT by Claire McNab. 208 pp. 4th Carol Ashton Mystery.
                                        ISBN 0-941483-84-3   10.95

THE BEVERLY MALIBU by Katherine V. Forrest. 288 pp. 3rd
Kate Delafield Mystery.   ISBN 0-941483-48-7   11.95

THE PROVIDENCE FILE by Amanda Kyle Williams. 256 pp.
2nd Madison McGuire Mystery.   ISBN 0-941483-92-4   8.95

I LEFT MY HEART by Jaye Maiman. 320 pp. 1st Robin Miller
Mystery.   ISBN 0-941483-72-X   10.95

THE PRICE OF SALT by Patricia Highsmith (writing as Claire
Morgan). 288 pp. Classic lesbian novel, first issued in 1952 . . .
acknowledged by its author under her own, very famous, name.
                                        ISBN 1-56280-003-5   10.95

SIDE BY SIDE by Isabel Miller. 256 pp. From beloved author of
Patience and Sarah.   ISBN 0-941483-77-0   10.95

STAYING POWER: LONG TERM LESBIAN COUPLES by
Susan E. Johnson. 352 pp. Joys of coupledom. ISBN 0-941-483-75-4   14.95

SLICK by Camarin Grae. 304 pp. Exotic, erotic adventure.
                                        ISBN 0-941483-74-6   9.95

NINTH LIFE by Lauren Wright Douglas. 256 pp. 2nd Caitlin
Reece Mystery.   ISBN 0-941483-50-9   9.95

PLAYERS by Robbi Sommers. 192 pp. Sizzling, erotic novel.
                                                   ISBN 0-941483-73-8   9.95

MURDER AT RED ROOK RANCH by Dorothy Tell. 224 pp.
1st Poppy Dillworth Mystery.   ISBN 0-941483-80-0   8.95

A ROOM FULL OF WOMEN by Elisabeth Nonas. 256 pp.
Contemporary Lesbian lives.   ISBN 0-941483-69-X   9.95

THEME FOR DIVERSE INSTRUMENTS by Jane Rule. 208 pp.
Powerful romantic lesbian stories.   ISBN 0-941483-63-0   8.95

CLUB 12 by Amanda Kyle Williams. 288 pp. Espionage thriller
featuring a lesbian agent!   ISBN 0-941483-64-9   9.95

DEATH DOWN UNDER by Claire McNab. 240 pp. 3rd Carol
Ashton Mystery.   ISBN 0-941483-39-8   10.95

MONTANA FEATHERS by Penny Hayes. 256 pp. Vivian and
Elizabeth find love in frontier Montana.   ISBN 0-941483-61-4   9.95

LIFESTYLES by Jackie Calhoun. 224 pp. Contemporary Lesbian
lives and loves.   ISBN 0-941483-57-6   10.95

WILDERNESS TREK by Dorothy Tell. 192 pp. Six women on
vacation learning "new" skills.   ISBN 0-941483-60-6   8.95

MURDER BY THE BOOK by Pat Welch. 256 pp. 1st Helen
Black Mystery.   ISBN 0-941483-59-2   9.95

THERE'S SOMETHING I'VE BEEN MEANING TO TELL YOU
Ed. by Loralee MacPike. 288 pp. Gay men and lesbians coming out
to their children.   ISBN 0-941483-44-4   9.95

LIFTING BELLY by Gertrude Stein. Ed. by Rebecca Mark. 104 pp.
Erotic poetry.   ISBN 0-941483-51-7   10.95

AFTER THE FIRE by Jane Rule. 256 pp. Warm, human novel by
this incomparable author.   ISBN 0-941483-45-2   8.95

PLEASURES by Robbi Sommers. 204 pp. Unprecedented
eroticism.   ISBN 0-941483-49-5   9.95

EDGEWISE by Camarin Grae. 372 pp. Spellbinding
adventure.   ISBN 0-941483-19-3   9.95

FATAL REUNION by Claire McNab. 224 pp. 2nd Carol Ashton
Mystery.   ISBN 0-941483-40-1   10.95

IN EVERY PORT by Karin Kallmaker. 228 pp. Jessica's sexy,
adventuresome travels.   ISBN 0-941483-37-7   10.95

OF LOVE AND GLORY by Evelyn Kennedy. 192 pp. Exciting
WWII romance.   ISBN 0-941483-32-0   10.95

CLICKING STONES by Nancy Tyler Glenn. 288 pp. Love
transcending time.   ISBN 0-941483-31-2   9.95

SOUTH OF THE LINE by Catherine Ennis. 216 pp. Civil War
adventure.   ISBN 0-941483-29-0   8.95

WOMAN PLUS WOMAN by Dolores Klaich. 300 pp. Supurb
Lesbian overview.   ISBN 0-941483-28-2   9.95

THE FINER GRAIN by Denise Ohio. 216 pp. Brilliant young
college lesbian novel.   ISBN 0-941483-11-8   8.95

BEFORE STONEWALL: THE MAKING OF A GAY AND
LESBIAN COMMUNITY by Andrea Weiss & Greta Schiller.
96 pp., 25 illus.   ISBN 0-941483-20-7   7.95

OSTEN'S BAY by Zenobia N. Vole. 204 pp. Sizzling adventure
romance set on Bonaire.   ISBN 0-941483-15-0   8.95

LESSONS IN MURDER by Claire McNab. 216 pp. 1st Carol Ashton
Mystery.   ISBN 0-941483-14-2   10.95

YELLOWTHROAT by Penny Hayes. 240 pp. Margarita, bandit,
kidnaps Julia.   ISBN 0-941483-10-X   8.95

SAPPHISTRY: THE BOOK OF LESBIAN SEXUALITY by
Pat Califia. 3d edition, revised. 208 pp.   ISBN 0-941483-24-X   10.95

CHERISHED LOVE by Evelyn Kennedy. 192 pp. Erotic Lesbian
love story.   ISBN 0-941483-08-8   10.95

THE SECRET IN THE BIRD by Camarin Grae. 312 pp. Striking,
psychological suspense novel.   ISBN 0-941483-05-3   8.95

TO THE LIGHTNING by Catherine Ennis. 208 pp. Romantic
Lesbian 'Robinson Crusoe' adventure.   ISBN 0-941483-06-1   8.95

DREAMS AND SWORDS by Katherine V. Forrest. 192 pp.
Romantic, erotic, imaginative stories.   ISBN 0-941483-03-7   10.95

MEMORY BOARD by Jane Rule. 336 pp. Memorable novel
about an aging Lesbian couple.   ISBN 0-941483-02-9   12.95

THE ALWAYS ANONYMOUS BEAST by Lauren Wright Douglas.
224 pp. 1st Caitlin Reece Mystery.
    ISBN 0-941483-04-5   8.95

MURDER AT THE NIGHTWOOD BAR by Katherine V. Forrest.
240 pp. 2nd Kate Delafield Mystery.   ISBN 0-930044-92-4   11.95

WINGED DANCER by Camarin Grae. 228 pp. Erotic Lesbian
adventure story.   ISBN 0-930044-88-6   8.95

PAZ by Camarin Grae. 336 pp. Romantic Lesbian adventurer
with the power to change the world.   ISBN 0-930044-89-4   8.95

SOUL SNATCHER by Camarin Grae. 224 pp. A puzzle, an
adventure, a mystery — Lesbian romance.   ISBN 0-930044-90-8   8.95

THE LOVE OF GOOD WOMEN by Isabel Miller. 224 pp.
Long-awaited new novel by the author of the beloved *Patience
and Sarah*.   ISBN 0-930044-81-9   8.95

THE LONG TRAIL by Penny Hayes. 248 pp. Vivid adventures
of two women in love in the old west.   ISBN 0-930044-76-2   8.95

AN EMERGENCE OF GREEN by Katherine V. Forrest. 288
pp. Powerful novel of sexual discovery.   ISBN 0-930044-69-X   11.95

THE LESBIAN PERIODICALS INDEX edited by Claire Potter.
432 pp. Author & subject index.   ISBN 0-930044-74-6   12.95

DESERT OF THE HEART by Jane Rule. 224 pp. A classic;
basis for the movie *Desert Hearts*.   ISBN 0-930044-73-8   10.95

SEX VARIANT WOMEN IN LITERATURE by Jeannette
Howard Foster. 448 pp. Literary history.   ISBN 0-930044-65-7   8.95

A HOT-EYED MODERATE by Jane Rule. 252 pp. Hard-hitting
essays on gay life; writing; art.   ISBN 0-930044-57-6   7.95

AMATEUR CITY by Katherine V. Forrest. 224 pp. 1st Kate
Delafield Mystery.   ISBN 0-930044-55-X   10.95

THE SOPHIE HOROWITZ STORY by Sarah Schulman. 176 pp.
Engaging novel of madcap intrigue.   ISBN 0-930044-54-1   7.95

THE YOUNG IN ONE ANOTHER'S ARMS by Jane Rule.
224 pp. Classic Jane Rule.   ISBN 0-930044-53-3   9.95

AGAINST THE SEASON by Jane Rule. 224 pp. Luminous,
complex novel of interrelationships.   ISBN 0-930044-48-7   8.95

LOVERS IN THE PRESENT AFTERNOON by Kathleen Fleming.
288 pp. A novel about recovery and growth.   ISBN 0-930044-46-0   8.95

CONTRACT WITH THE WORLD by Jane Rule. 340 pp. Powerful, panoramic novel of gay life.   ISBN 0-930044-28-2   9.95

THIS IS NOT FOR YOU by Jane Rule. 284 pp. A letter to a
beloved is also an intricate novel.   ISBN 0-930044-25-8   8.95

OUTLANDER by Jane Rule. 207 pp. Short stories and essays by
one of our finest writers.   ISBN 0-930044-17-7   8.95

These are just a few of the many Naiad Press titles — we are the oldest and
largest lesbian/feminist publishing company in the world. We also offer an
enormous selection of lesbian video products. Please request a complete
catalog. We offer personal service; we encourage and welcome direct mail
orders from individuals who have limited access to bookstores carrying our
publications.